You're invited to
event: Kingsley Ec
Auction.

New on the auction block this year is Daniel, a
wealthy widower and dominant. However, he hap-
pens to have his eyes on another first-timer in the
club's auction: Anya, a strikingly beautiful virgin
submissive from his native Canada.

Too bad Anya hates him on sight. Or does she?
There's a fine line between hatred and burning
passion, and Daniel is determined to bring Anya
across it. Now let the bidding begin...

THE ORIGINAL SINNERS PULP LIBRARY

Vintage paperback-inspired edi-
tions of standalone novels and
novellas from *USA Today* best-
seller Tiffany Reisz's million-
copy selling Original Sinners
erotic romance series. Learn
more at tiffanyreisz.com.

THE ORIGINAL SINNERS
PULP LIBRARY

THE AUCTION

IMMERSED IN PLEASURE and

SUBMIT TO DESIRE

THE LAST GOOD KNIGHT

LITTLE RED RIDING CROP

MISCHIEF

THE MISTRESS FILES

The Auction

The Auction

TIFFANY REISZ

8TH CIRCLE PRESS • LOUISVILLE, KY

Un-edited, rough draft parts of this book were previously made available for preview as *Daniel Part Two* on TiffanyReisz.com

Cover design by Andrew Shaffer

Front cover image contains a photo used under license from iStock by Getty Images. Interior images licensed from Shutterstock.com.

Mass-Market Paperback ISBN: 978-1-949769-22-7

Also available as an ebook and audiobook from 8th Circle Press

First Edition

AUTHOR'S NOTE

The Auction *takes place approximately one year after the Original Sinners novella* The Gift *(aka* Seven Day Loan).

The Auction—*like all of the Original Sinners Pulp Library titles—can be read as a standalone story.*

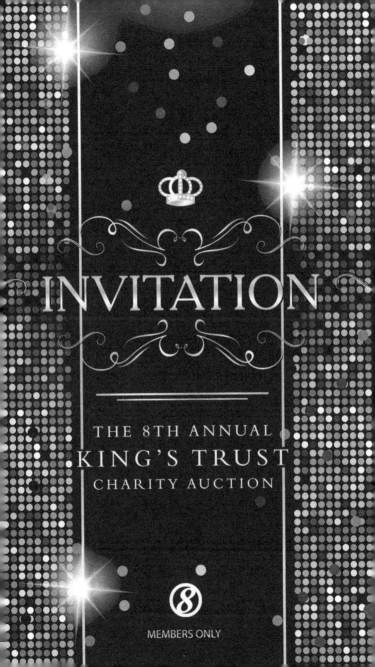

1

For the life of him, Daniel couldn't put his finger on the reason he'd chosen this house of all places as his first stop upon returning to America.

Exhausted and bedraggled, with his eight-hundred-dollar hiking boots still crusted with dirt from Machu Picchu, he should have been anywhere but standing in front of one of Manhattan's most luxurious townhouses. Four stories? Five? Plus, a coveted Riverside Drive address. White exterior with sleek black trim, imposing black iron fence... The townhouse was the public face of a very private world, one that Daniel used to belong to but wasn't sure if he did anymore, wasn't even sure if he wanted to belong anymore. Still, nice place. No, not nice. What had Eleanor called it? After a year and a half, he hoped his brain had relinquished that little memory, finally.

Swanky. She'd called Kingsley Edge's infamous townhouse "swanky." And he still remembered it.

Annoyed with himself—were scientists ever going to invent a cure for hopeless romanticism?— he passed through the wrought-iron gate and mounted the steps. He rang the doorbell and waited. Not surprisingly, a young woman of shocking beauty opened the door. Dark red hair, wide amber eyes, and ripe red lips...

"May I help you, *monsieur*?" the girl asked. Her wide eyes looked too innocent to be part of this infamous household.

The girl spoke with an accent, one he recognized all too well. French but not French. The inside of his cheek twitched.

Her eyes flashed at him. "Something funny?"

Prickly little thing. Kingsley always did like his women temperamental—it was more fun to punish them when they'd earned it.

"Nothing at all," Daniel said. "Sorry. Just amused Monsieur 'If You Aren't From Paris, You Aren't Really French' picked a *Québécoise* for his doorkeeper."

She raised her chin and glared at him. "He must have someone standing guard to keep you English Canadians out."

Smart girl, or a good guess? Either that or his knee-jerk "sorry" must have given him away. Once a Canadian, always a Canadian. Even after twenty years living in the States.

"He won't mind me," Daniel said. "Is our Lord of the Underground home?"

"Might be. Might not. Depends on who you are. And from the looks of you, I would say...*non*, the master isn't home."

The looks of him? Ah, Miss Quebec might have had a point there. From South America, he'd flown straight to New York City. Yesterday he'd been in Peru. Today, Manhattan. He was wearing faded jeans to match his battered boots, a khaki long-sleeved t-shirt, and scratched wraparound Ray-Bans—the same clothes he'd had on yesterday. Add on two days of stubble, a weather-beaten tan, and sun-faded hair badly in need of a cut, and he knew he looked nothing like the usual type who knocked on this door.

"Would you mind checking? *S'il vous plait*?" he added, hoping the French didn't sound too sarcastic. He was going for "just sarcastic enough."

The girl exhaled dramatically. "If he is home, whom shall I say is calling?"

"Just tell him it's Daniel. He knows me."

The girl raised her eyebrow and regarded him coldly. She nodded at the front steps. "You wait *here*...Daniel."

The girl closed the door in his face and Daniel almost laughed. Gone for only a day, and he already missed South America and its complete dearth of ill-tempered red-headed doorkeepers.

The door opened once more. The girl gave him a look of such disgust that he forgot for a moment she wasn't actually French.

"You can come in," she said as she stepped back and let him inside the house. "But wipe your boots. Or better, take them off. Then burn them."

Daniel started to brush past her but paused mid-step. Something, some of the old mischief stopped him. And that rudeness of hers demanded a little punishment.

He faced the girl, pushed his sunglasses on top of his head, and gave her a hard blue-eyed stare, the stare his late wife had called The Ouch. Maggie knew when he looked at her like that, gave her The Ouch, she'd have trouble walking the next day...

His grumpy little doorkeeper returned The Ouch with a vicious glare of her own. But Daniel knew a sub when he saw one. In Kingsley's household, one found only three types of people: dominants, submissives, and the rare, elusive switch. Her little pale blue sailor dress and lace-trimmed ankle socks did not scream "dominatrix" to him. Their staring contest was no contest. The Ouch won every time. After a few seconds, she lowered her eyes to the floor. He took a step forward. She took a step back. Her cheeks flushed and her lips reddened. If he wasn't mistaken, even her breathing quickened.

"That's better," he said softly. "Do you have a name?"

She raised her eyes, smiled, undefeated. "Yes."

"And it is?"

She leaned in close and whispered, "Celine Dion."

Before he could reply, he heard another voice. He turned around.

"It cannot be...is our Daniel finally out of the lion's den?"

The voice belonged to the tall, dark-haired, dark-eyed man descending the stairs in a suit like something off the cover of an old romance novel. The man's riding boots were polished. Daniel had once asked if he did a lot of riding. *Not horses,* the man had said.

"Kingsley Edge," Daniel said without smiling. "Were you quoting the Bible? I didn't think you'd ever heard of it."

Kingsley shrugged elegantly and rolled his eyes. Unlike the testy doorkeeper, he was true blue, white, and red French and had the attitude, the accent, and the libido to prove it.

"Blame the priest," Kingsley said. "He's still trying to save my soul. I keep telling him I don't have one."

Daniel's smile faded as Kingsley met him at the bottom of the steps. "He's not here, is he?"

Movement in the music room caught Daniel's eye. He saw a few beautiful women lounging about two very lucky and handsome young men. But no priests in residence. Thank God. Daniel wasn't quite ready for that conversation yet.

"Sunday afternoon," Kingsley said and motioned Daniel to follow him back upstairs. "He's either praying right now or reminding his little pet what his cock tastes like."

"I don't think she needs reminding," added the doorkeeper.

Kingsley exhaled, turned to the girl and said something in rapid French. In equally rapid but far testier French she replied. Finally Kingsley raised his hand, snapped his fingers, and pointed at the hallway. The girl gave Kingsley a mock curtsy before spinning on her heel and storming away. Her skirt lifted with that tempestuous twirl, and Daniel caught a glimpse of white lace-trimmed panties. She should flounce away more often.

"You're keeping a *Québécoise* as a pet these days?" Daniel asked.

"She's part of my Imperial Collection. I'm creating the New French Empire...one beautiful girl at a time." Kingsley started up the stairs and Daniel followed.

"No boys?"

"Are you enlisting?"

"You're not my type."

"*Pfft*," he said, *très français*. "I'm everyone's type." He waved his hand.

As they walked, Kingsley whistled "La Marseillaise," the French national anthem. The whistling always made Daniel nervous. No man alive worked so diligently to cultivate an air so casual. Daniel knew better. So when Kingsley ushered him into his private office, and Daniel found his back pressed to the door and a hand on his throat, he wasn't particularly surprised.

He stayed calm and didn't fight back. Coming here had been a risk, and for the life of him he still couldn't say exactly why he'd decided to take it.

At first neither man said anything. Kingsley's dark eyes bored into Daniel's blue ones. Kingsley was rakishly handsome and had half the women in New York at his feet. Quite a few of the men, too. Yet underneath the playboy exterior lurked an extremely dangerous man. Dangerously intelligent. Dangerously loyal.

Dangerously loyal to the man whose lover Daniel had tried to steal last year.

Hence the chokehold.

————

"WHATEVER HAPPENED TO, 'WELCOME HOME?'"

"This is your welcome home." Kingsley grinned and tightened the hold, but only a little. They were friends, after all.

"I guess Eleanor told you."

"She told me. You know the rules, *mon ami*. We may borrow another's toys, pet another's pet...but we do not steal another's property."

Daniel took a shallow breath. As hard as Kingsley was holding his neck, a deep breath wasn't an option. "There's no stealing Eleanor. I asked her to stay. There's a difference."

"You are alive. Obviously there's a difference."

Kingsley released Daniel's throat and backed away. He collapsed into a leather armchair in front of his desk. "*Et vive la différence, oui?*"

Daniel rubbed his throat as he sat in the chair opposite Kingsley. "Right. Yeah. *Vive la différence.*"

Kingsley laughed his low, sardonic laugh. The laugh died. Kingsley narrowed his eyes at him.

"Why did you come back here, Daniel? If you're planning on trying again with her...I wouldn't recommend it."

Daniel stretched out his tired legs. "I've been asking myself that question since my plane landed. I don't know. Tired of traveling. Not ready to go home yet. Plus...I wanted to thank you."

"Thank me? For what?"

Leaning forward, Daniel clasped his hands between his knees. His hands...once they'd been smooth as a woman's. He'd been an archivist in his old life and the worst thing that ever happened to his hands was the occasional paper cut. Now for a year and a half he'd been scrambling up mountains, trekking through rain forests, and digging through ancient ruins. His hands looked it.

"The funeral," Daniel said. "I would never have been able to forgive myself if I hadn't gone to the funeral."

The funeral. Maggie's funeral. His late wife. He'd only made it through that day because Kingsley had given him drugs. The good kind. He'd half-joked to Eleanor that Kingsley had slipped him a horse tranquilizer. It might have been, actually. Whatever it was, it had done the job. On a normal day, such a drug would have put him on his back for a week. That day, it had merely disconnected his mind from his body and allowed him to stay vertical for those two necessary, nightmarish hours.

"It pays to have a well-stocked medicine cabinet. And liquor cabinet. Can I get you something from either of them now?"

Daniel smiled. "No. I'm fine. Thank you. I should probably go before you-know-who shows up."

"He won't kill you. He's a pacifist."

"And a sadist."

Kingsley smiled. "Who isn't? Look, he won. He knows he won. He always knew he'd win, or he wouldn't have sent her to you in the first place. I'd be more afraid of her than him, if I were you."

"Elle's going to beat me up, too?"

"Not your body, but your heart. Again. She does have that power over men."

"I noticed."

Understatement of the century. Kingsley peered at him, as if trying to see in Daniel's eyes if he was still in love with Eleanor or if he'd come to his senses.

"I hadn't left my house in three years," Daniel said. "I still can't believe that sometimes. When every day feels the same, three years can pass in a blink. I think I might have died in that house if she hadn't dragged me out."

Daniel had only had Eleanor for one week—a gift, of sorts. Or, to be more accurate, a loan, since he'd had to give her back. But she came and worked her magic on him and when she left, so did he. She'd joked about Tierra del Fuego. Why? Who knew, with her. She probably just liked saying the name. So after three years exiled in his own home, he went there for one reason and one reason alone—to send her a damn postcard postmarked from Tierra del Fuego to prove he was free again.

But was he truly free? He couldn't escape thinking of her. Maybe not as free as he wanted. Not yet.

"Anyway, it was good to see you again, King. Apart from the manslaughter attempt." Daniel started to stand but the door burst open and two laughing women nearly fell into the room.

"Tessa! Irina!" Kingsley glared at them both. "Come here. Now."

Kingsley pointed at the floor. Both women pasted on artificial looks of contrition as they simpered across the Persian rug and sat at Kingsley's feet.

"Ladies," Kingsley began, "what are you two doing? Or do I not want to know? Tessa —answer me."

He tapped the buxom olive-skinned girl on the tip of her nose. "Anya said you were in your office with the ugliest man she'd ever seen in her life. We had to see for ourselves."

"She's such a liar," said the hazel-eyed brunette glancing at Daniel. "He's more handsome than you are, King."

Kingsley gasped and put his hand over his chest in melodramatic shock. "Blasphemy, Irina." He pulled Irina's earlobe. "No one is more handsome than I am."

"You're too pretty," the girl continued, flashing her eyes at Daniel. He couldn't take his eyes off the girl. Irina spoke beautifully clear English but with a tinge of a Russian accent. She, too, must have been part of Kingsley's Imperial Collection. "He looks rough, rugged. I like his eyes."

"Rough?" Kingsley scoffed. "I spent four years in the French Foreign Legion. I have bullet wounds. That," Kingsley pointed at Daniel, "is a librarian."

"Archivist," Daniel corrected. Ex-archivist actually. He inherited a huge sum of money from his late wife and hadn't worked in years. Now at thirty-eight he felt restless, useless. Being a man of leisure didn't really suit him. He knew he needed something else in his life again. Just didn't know what yet.

"Intelligent men are my favorite," Irina said, nearly purring the words. "And in such rare supply these days."

Kingsley exhaled dramatically and snapped his fingers. Both women stood up. The Russian Irina cast another lascivious glance at Daniel.

"I'm extremely smart," Kingsley countered.

"Except around women. Now go before I'm forced to punish both of you for eavesdropping. And tell Anya to behave herself. Grand prize or not, I'll turn her over my knee if I have to. I'll turn her over my knee even if I don't have to."

"Yes, sir," both women responded as they shuffled toward the door, pretending to be chastened.

"Irina?" Kingsley called out. He waved her back over to him. Kingsley reached up and wrapped a hand around the back of Irina's neck and pulled her ear to his lips. He whispered something to her and she nodded, turned her head and whispered back. Daniel sighed. The whispering was one of his least favorite of the dominant tricks. He could be telling the girl to fetch his dry-cleaning for all Daniel knew. Probably was. But by whispering it to her, he created a little secret society that only he and Irina belonged to. Doms did that all the time in Kingsley's world. Such a mindfuck. Back in his days as a dominant, Daniel usually avoided the mindfuck. Why waste time fucking the mind when he could be fucking the body?

Irina kissed Kingsley on the cheek, glanced once more at Daniel, and left the room.

"Are you sure you won't stay for lunch?" Kingsley asked.

"No thanks. Not hungry." Not for food anyway. Being around all of Kingsley's beautiful submissives had him thinking things he'd long ago tried to push out of his mind. "I should go. Haven't been home yet. I know you're busy." Daniel rose from his chair.

"I'll have Anya see you out. She'll hate me for it." Kingsley went to the door.

"Anya? That would be your ill-tempered doorkeeper?"

"Daughter of *Quebecois* separatists. She loathes Canadians. Don't take her hatred of you personally. I'd punish her for how rude she was to you, but she's off-limits, unfortunately."

"Off-limits? What woman in the world is off-limits to you?"

"The auction's in a month. She's *Le Grand Prix.*"

Daniel's eyes widened. "You're still doing the auction? The FBI hasn't shut it down yet?"

Kingsley waved his hand dismissively. "The FBI is always welcome at my auction. It's for charity after all."

Daniel snorted a laugh. Charity? Technically Kingsley did donate a large portion of the proceeds to some Catholic charity for the poor. He took his usual fifteen percent, however. Kingsley's auction happened every August and was the talk of the town. Ostensibly, it appeared to be just another silly fundraiser for the rich and bored. Attractive people auctioned themselves off for dates with the highest bidder. But these weren't your average attractive nobodies. They were highly trained submissives and dominants. And the "dates" weren't dates. No dinner and a movie for the highest bidder. They won sex—hardcore kinky sex with the beautiful deviant of their dreams.

"So your doorkeeper is the Grand Prize? I pity whoever wins her," Daniel said. "She's beautiful, but the personality could use a little work."

"They won't be bidding on her personality," Kingsley said. "They're bidding on her virginity."

Daniel only stared at Kingsley.

"You'd be ill-tempered too if you were still a virgin at twenty-four," Kingsley said. "The last time we had a virgin in the auction, the highest bid went into six figures. Most we'd ever made off one person."

Kingsley winked at him as he opened the door for Daniel. He continued, "Now are you sure I can't get you anything? Something to eat, to drink? I feel so inhospitable threatening your life without even lunch after."

"I'm really fine. I think." Daniel's mind still boggled. Anya, the temperamental doorkeeper, not just a virgin but a prize virgin up for auction... Kingsley lived in a very different world than the rest of the unwashed masses.

"Perhaps something stronger than lunch," Kingsley said as he veered off onto the second floor instead of heading down to the entrance. Daniel narrowed his eyes and followed. "Perhaps a little of this is what you need before you go."

Kingsley stopped in front of a door and opened it. Looking in, Daniel saw Irina, the beautiful Russian brunette, naked on the bed, kneeling in submissive silence, her long dark hair flowing like water down her back.

All day long Daniel had been trying to put his finger on the reason why, of all places, he'd come to Kingsley's first when coming back to America.

Now he put his finger right on it.

Kingsley said, "Welcome home."

2

At his side, Kingsley smirked while Daniel stared at Irina and considered the offer.

It wasn't as if he'd been celibate this past year while traveling. Although Daniel's heart remained faithful to the girl he'd spent one perfect week with, his body had demanded more than bittersweet memories. He'd had lovers—several of them—during his travels in South America. Vanilla trysts only. He'd never felt close enough to the women or safe enough to reveal the real Daniel to them. So while the sex—passionate and rough—had satisfied his physical hunger, his soul craved more.

Still, any gift offered by Kingsley Edge usually came with strings attached. Or ropes. And yet...

This is what he'd wanted. Otherwise, he wouldn't have come here.

"Anything I should know?" Daniel asked. His heart raced a little faster, his blood warmed.

"She's well-trained. Her safe word is 'Stalin.'"

"Stalin? Really?"

"Nothing kills the mood faster than bringing a genocidal maniac into the bedroom. She's not in love with pain, but don't be afraid to be..." Kingsley paused for effect. "...*thorough*."

"Thorough," Daniel repeated, the word causing his groin to tighten pleasantly.

"Enjoy your lunch. I've already had mine."

"Then what's that?" Daniel nodded to the end of the hall where a young man—pale and handsome and at least ten years Kingsley's junior—waited outside the door to the master bedroom.

"Dessert."

Kingsley and his dessert disappeared into the room, leaving Daniel alone with Irina.

He stepped into the bedroom and shut the door behind him.

For a full minute, he stood directly behind Irina so he couldn't see her face. Her hair was a shade too light and the body a bit too willowy, but if he wanted, he could almost pretend this beautiful submissive was...

No. He stopped his thoughts in their tracks. He'd done that to Eleanor the first time they'd had sex. He'd closed his eyes, pretended he had Maggie back. Now he regretted the lost memory of his first time with her.

"Irina. Russian, right?"

"Yes, sir."

Sir. Was there a word in the world sweeter to his ears than that one? And to hear it in a soft but slightly sinister Russian accent sent a little thrill of satisfaction through his entire body.

"My mother's family was Polish. Fled their home country during the war. Do you want to guess why?"

"Better weather, sir?" she asked, a tremor in her voice that might have been a laugh in disguise.

Daniel grinned at the back of her head. He took a step toward the bed, then another. He gathered a fistful of her long dark hair and held it firmly.

"They were fleeing the Russian Army." He brought his mouth to her ear. "But don't worry. I won't hold it against you."

"You can if you want to."

He almost laughed. Kingsley did know how to pick them, didn't he?

Slowly he ran his fingers up and down the column on her spine. Such smooth, soft skin. Unmarked, untouched... She hadn't been beaten in a long time. Not a professional submissive then. An enthusiastic amateur, he hoped.

"I usually don't beat a woman on a first date." He forced her head to the side and exposed her neck. Gently he bit at the pulse point beneath her ear.

"I wouldn't worry about that, sir. It's not a date."

Daniel laughed softly in her ear.

If he trusted himself enough, he'd cover her from neck to ankles in welts. But he hadn't played with pain in a long time, and he worried he'd cross the line if he let himself go. Maybe soon, but not yet.

Instead, Daniel assaulted her neck and sculpted shoulder with kisses. He traced a line with his fingers from her neck, over each full breast, and down her stomach. Cupping her gently between the legs, Daniel fondled her smooth bare labia, stoking the heat coming from inside her. He found her clitoris with his fingertip and kneaded it gently.

Irina inhaled sharply, and he gave her ear a quick nibble before pulling away and leaving her panting.

Daniel glanced around the room. He'd never played in here before, but that wouldn't be a problem. He already knew where everything was. Next to the bed—king-size, of course, as everything in Kingsley's townhouse was king-sized—he found a crystal bowl filled with an assortment of condoms. Under the bed, he found three large leather suitcases, color-coded. Silver for bondage. Black for sex toys. White for pain. He wanted the white case but pulled out the silver case instead. Maybe he wasn't ready for the crops and floggers yet, but he'd been rappelling up and down mountainsides for months. Ropes and knots? That he could handle.

He didn't speak to Irina as he dug through the silver case. With her face away from him, she couldn't see what he was doing, what he was choosing. Daniel bit back a smug grin—okay, so maybe he did like a little mindfuck after all.

From the case, he pulled out a length of black silk rope, one set of ankle cuffs, and a two-foot spreader bar. He tossed the bar and the cuffs on the bed—he wouldn't need those until later.

"King said you like it thorough. What don't you like?"

"Time wasting. Sir."

Russian women, Daniel was learning, were their own breed.

Without asking permission, he pushed Irina onto her stomach and wove the rope around both wrists behind her back. Tempting as it was to hog-tie her for her arrogance, he decided against it. He might strain her back too much. That hadn't been a concern with Eleanor, who wasn't just petite but had a rather accommodating body. Extremely accommodating.

After tying up Irina, he stopped to look at her. Was there anything in the world more erotic than a woman who'd given herself up entirely into his hands? His power? Her trust? A potent combination.

Once more, he ran his hands over her body, down her arms, through her long hair. He even stroked the soles of her feet, making her twitch and flinch. His cock had hardened almost painfully as he'd bound her. Now it pressed against the zipper of his jeans, aching to be released.

He hoped his and Kingsley's definition of thorough were the same.

With two quick movements, he had Irina off the bed and onto her knees in front of him. He gripped the back of her neck with his left hand while his right hand opened his pants. He let the tip of his cock lightly touch her waiting lips.

He didn't have to give her the order to take him into her mouth. Without hesitation, she wrapped her lips around him and sucked deep. His hand tightened on her neck hard enough he knew he risked leaving bruises. She didn't seem to mind.

With careful undulations of his hips, he thrust into her mouth. God, it felt like the first time he'd had real sex since Eleanor left him. During his vanilla encounters, his body had been on autopilot. Now the real Daniel was waking up, coming back to life again.

Even as a dominant, he always considered himself a gentleman. He never inflicted pain without offering equal or greater pleasure to his submissive. His hand slid from Irina's neck to her breasts, and he toyed with her nipples...gently at first and then with greater intensity as she began to moan with need. The moaning caused the back of her throat to vibrate. Daniel breathed in deep and forced himself not to come immediately.

God, he'd missed this.

He pulled out of her mouth. With practiced ease, he untied the knots and released Irina.

"Feet on the floor, face the bed." He snapped

his fingers and pointed right at the spot where he wanted her.

"Yes, sir."

She obeyed quickly but without undue haste—eager, not afraid. Daniel walked to the opposite side of the bed and crooked his finger at Irina, a silent command for her to lean forward and stretch her arms out toward him. He knotted the rope around her wrists, then tied the other end to the bed frame. She pulled hard, testing the strength of his restraints. Those knots of his had kept him alive two thousand meters above sea level. They'd undoubtedly hold one woman to a bed. And no chance either the bed frame would break or bend. Not any bed that belonged to Kingsley Edge. His beds would survive the Apocalypse.

Pleased with her position, Daniel returned to Irina. He tapped the back of her knee, signaling her to bend her leg like a horse being shoed. Except he was buckling the ankle cuffs onto her legs. Then, with two snap hooks, he secured her ankles to the two-foot spreader bar. Once finished, he took a few steps back to admire his captive Russian. In her current posture, she could hide nothing of herself from him. He drank in the sight of her long naked back, long legs trapped in cuffs, and her beautiful damp pussy, slightly open, beckoning him.

"Arch your back," he ordered. Standing directly behind her, Daniel caressed Irina's back, her bottom, hips, and thighs. He touched her gently, lightly, until she groaned with frustration.

Then with the full force of every muscle in his arm, he slapped the back of her upper thigh.

Irina gave an utterly shocked and satisfying yelp of pain. He glanced down and saw a bright red handprint rising on her skin.

Daniel stretched across her back and pressed his mouth to her ear. "That was for the 'better weather' joke."

Irina didn't answer. She'd still feel that hit to-morrow with every step she took.

"Say you're sorry, and I won't do it again...today."

"I'm sorry, sir."

"Good girl." Daniel stood and massaged the red and burning welt. "I aimed for the thigh on purpose. The skin on the ass is a little too thick. The thighs hurt more. Can you tell the difference?"

He slapped her thigh again, right on the red spot, and reared back and spanked her ass, once, sharply, the sound echoing like a gunshot. Irina flinched and cried out both times. Daniel could have patted himself on the back. He might be out of practice, but he still had it.

Daniel moved his hand to the apex of her thighs. Once more, he found her clitoris and kneaded it. He felt the heat of her against his hand, a heat that drew him in. He pushed a single finger inside her and let the wet warmth envelop him.

"Kingsley said you weren't in love with pain. As wet as you are, I might have to argue with him."

She breathed hard as he pushed a second finger into her pussy. "I was that wet before you hit me, sir."

"Were you? And why is that?"

"Because—" she began and stopped for another breath as he pushed in a third finger. His cock pulsed as her muscles contracted around his hand. "Because...I want you to fuck me, sir."

Daniel smiled at her prone and helpless body. "You aren't the first woman who's ever said that to me. But since I've never heard it in a Russian accent before, I'm tempted to do just that."

"Please, sir," she begged. He loved that note of desperation in her voice, that hunger. He'd missed kinky women so much.

He reached into the bowl by the bed and pulled out a condom. Within seconds he had it on. Slowly he pushed into her wet heat, filling her one inch at a time.

She groaned loudly and gripped the ropes that bound her as Daniel held onto her hips and began thrusting. He took slow, deep breaths and concentrated on the elegant lines of Irina's long back, the way the sunlight turned her hair almost red. He focused on anything but the excruciating pleasure of being inside this beautiful submissive. Otherwise, he'd come before he really got to enjoy her.

Irina's tight vagina contracted around him as

her body neared orgasm. It nearly killed him to pull out, but he did it.

After all, Kingsley had said she liked it "thorough."

Daniel snapped open the black case which held the sex toys and pulled out a vibrator and one of several tubes of lube.

"Do you have any problems with anal?" he asked.

"Only that most men are terrible at it."

"I'm not most men." He spread lube over himself and then into her—filling her with the cool, wet liquid until she was slick and open and ready for him.

A soft moan escaped his lips as he carefully penetrated her ass. He didn't thrust, however. Not yet. He took the vibrator off the bed, turned it on, and started to push it inside Irina.

She gasped and buried her face into the bedspread. Daniel let her ragged breathing guide him as he continued to press it deeper in her.

"Can you take both?" he asked, brushing her hair off her face. For all he loved sensual torture, he'd stop in a heartbeat if he was actually hurting her.

"Yes." She gasped the word. "Please."

At the "please," he kissed the side of her face. No more did he force himself to hold back. He thrust now, hard and deep, riding her with long strokes. With every push, she gasped. He could feel the thrumming through the thin wall that separated him from the vibrator. His eyes nearly watered from the need to come. But he held back, dug his hands deeper into her skin, and kept pushing.

"Sir?" was all Irina could say.

"Come," he ordered, and with a hoarse cry, Irina let go. Her entire body shuddered. She groaned something in Russian, and the one part of his brain that was still functioning reminded him to ask her later what she'd said, if she remembered.

Daniel closed his eyes as his climax overtook him. He'd fought it off so long that when he came, it felt like the orgasm would never end.

A grunt of discomfort from underneath him brought Daniel back to himself. Carefully he took the vibrator out of Irina, then pulled out. He left her where she was, spent, with her ankles still bound by the spreader bar while he disposed of the condom. Finally, he released her.

With a tired smile, Irina stood and faced him, wrapped her arms around his neck.

"Thank you, sir."

Daniel ran his hands from her wrists to her shoulders, pushed her onto her back, and straddled her thighs. He pulled off his shirt and threw it on the floor. He climbed onto Irina, pinning her to the mattress.

———

AFTER TWO HOURS OF PLAYING, Daniel finally gave up and crawled from the bed. He felt as tired as he had after scaling Aconcagua in Argentina two months ago. Just as tired, just as exuberant.

"You don't have to do that, you know," Irina said as Daniel pulled his jeans back on and buttoned them.

"What?"

"Put on clothes. Clothes on is not a good look for you. Clothes off is better."

Irina lay on her side, watching him with that same lascivious look she'd given him in Kingsley's upstairs office. Daniel decided that was what he missed most about being around women in the BDSM scene. Vanilla women wanted flirting, seduction, the whole song and dance. He got so bored with the dishonesty. He needed a woman who simply asked for what she wanted—especially if what she wanted was him. Never had that been a problem with Maggie, and certainly not with Eleanor. She had whispered a few things in his ear that had made even him almost blush.

"What's her name?"

Daniel tensed but didn't answer at first. He found his shirt and tugged it over his head. "Who?" he asked.

"The girl in your eyes."

Daniel sat on the edge of the bed. Irina propped herself up on a pillow, not bothering to pull a sheet over her bare breasts. Shamelessness was a superb quality in a woman.

"I don't think I could see if I had a girl in my eyes."

Irina raised her hand and ran her fingers through his hair, which desperately needed cutting. "What's her name?"

Nothing good would come of answering her question. But Irina had given herself to him and held nothing back. He owed her the same.

"Eleanor."

Irina's eyes widened. "You don't mean *his* Eleanor, do you?"

Daniel gave a low rueful laugh. *His* Eleanor. No name required. "You know her?"

"Everyone knows the White Queen."

"The White Queen? Is that what you all call her behind her back?"

Irina shrugged. "Or to her face. It makes her laugh. Everything makes her laugh. She wears a white collar, you know, just like his. And she wears white all the time. If you ask her why she'll say it shows the blood better. She's demonic." Irina made it sound like a compliment.

"She was an angel to me."

"Are you sure we're talking about the same girl?" Irina asked, grinning.

"I suppose she was a bit rougher around the edges than the usual sub."

"That girl," Irina said, slipping out from under the sheets, "is no sub."

Daniel stared at Irina as she took her clothes

from the back of a chair and started to dress. "What do you mean?"

"There are submissives...and there are people who submit. She's the latter. I have met sadists less intimidating than she is. I say she's either a dominant in denial or a switch waiting to switch. But how do you know her? I've never seen you here before. I'd remember you. "He smiled at the compliment.

"I'm from before your time," Daniel admitted. He felt older than his thirty-eight years. "Her owner and I used to play chess together, here, a long time ago." Not that long, really. Ten years ago? Felt like a thousand. "Long games, deep into the night, talking about everything while he wiped the floor with me. We were good friends, if you can believe it."

"I can believe it. He's, you know, a little scary until you talk to him for five minutes, then you realize you can trust him with your life. She is the one who worries me." Irina winked.

It was surprising to hear that his Eleanor had this reputation. He'd found her whimsical and sexy, smart and a little wild, but Irina made her sound almost dangerous. Had she kept that side from him? Or had he just not seen it? Not wanted to see it?

"As much as I hate the man now, I suppose I do owe him. I was in a bad place after my wife died, and I was in it for years. He sent me Eleanor for a week...a week's worth of therapy."

"Shock therapy?"

Daniel laughed. Shock therapy, yes. He ordered her to do things, and she'd obey, sometimes after laughing in his face. She even told him that compared to her real master, Daniel was about as scary as a baby bunny. In her eyes, Daniel had glimpsed anger, desire, hunger, amusement, but never fear. Not once. Maybe Irina was onto something.

But no, no way. When she submitted to him, angels sang and the heavens opened.

"Submissives should be strong," Daniel said. "They have to be. I don't think she's a dominant or a switch, just the perfect submissive."

"You want to bet on that?"

"No dominant could submit as well as she did."

"Really?" Irina asked as she pulled on her black blouse and buttoned it over her breasts. "How do you think I just did?"

Irina shoved her feet into her boots and gave him a waiting look. Daniel remained speechless.

Irina patted him on the side of the face in a manner so patronizing he knew he'd just tied up, spanked, and fucked a fellow dominant.

She flicked open her tiny purse and handed him a card. Solid black, silver ink. *Mistress Irina,* followed by a phone number. Not just a dominant, but a dominatrix.

"Call me. Next time I'll make you beg for it, little boy."

3

Irina kissed him goodbye and left the bedroom. Daniel finished dressing. When he stepped into the hall, he found Kingsley lounging in an armchair, smoking. He blew a smoke ring and pushed two fingers through the hole. Very subtle.

Daniel crossed his arms and leaned against the doorframe. "Last I remember, you were trying to quit."

"I am trying. Just not very hard." Kingsley stubbed out the cigarette in an ashtray. "Did you enjoy your lunch?"

Daniel glared at Kingsley as he slowly rose from the chair. "She's a dominatrix."

"So? I like all the dominants on my payroll to bottom every now and then," Kingsley said. "It's good for them. Humbling. Especially when I'm doing the humbling."

Kingsley waved his hand, and Daniel followed him downstairs.

"You used to be a pro dom," Daniel reminded him.

Kingsley raised his eyebrow at him as they reached the landing. "Daniel, I can't imagine what you're implying."

"*Monsieur*," came a sharp but sweet voice from the bottom of the steps. Anya again. Kingsley walked down the steps to the foyer, where Anya met him with a sheaf of messages. To Kingsley, Anya gave a curtsy. To Daniel, a look of pure loathing. Daniel hated knowing the girl was both virginal and off-limits. Every time she looked at him like that, he mentally put another handprint on her ass.

Kingsley dismissed her in French. To him, she gave another curtsy. To Daniel, another look of pure loathing. She flounced off again, the skirt of her sailor dress flying up as she twirled away.

"I know what you're thinking..." Kingsley sang as he glanced through his messages.

"No, you don't."

"You want to make our little sailor girl walk your plank."

Daniel smiled. "Okay, maybe you do know what I'm thinking. I guess I'm on her eternal shit list for being Canadian. Who hates Canadians anyway? We're nice. We're legally required to be nice." He watched as she disappeared down the long hallway.

"She doesn't hate you because you're Canadian. She hates you because you dress for shit."

Daniel looked down at his clothes. "I was in a Peruvian airport yesterday. Was I supposed to wear a tux?"

Kingsley tossed the messages onto a table and gave him a long look. "You're not in Peru anymore, my friend. I'll call my tailor. You go see him tomorrow."

Daniel exhaled heavily. None of his old clothes fit very well anymore. Although he'd always been in good shape, a year of climbing mountains had broadened his shoulders and shrunk his waistline. And Kingsley did have the best tailor in town.

"I hadn't planned on a long stay in the city," Daniel reminded him. He had his country house to check on, too. Not that he particularly relished going back there. Too many memories waited for him—memories of the last year with Maggie as he watched her die, three years of hell after she'd gone, and one week of bliss when Eleanor came to him.

"Change your plans. At least stay in town through the auction. It's in two weeks."

"Why?" Daniel asked. He had no intention whatsoever of bidding on Anya. Not even to terrify her with the very idea of giving up her virginity to a poorly-dressed English-speaking Canadian.

Kingsley slapped him on the arm, and then took a cigarette case out of his jacket pocket and shook one out. "Because you're in it, *mon ami.*"

"I'm what?"

"You think there's such a thing as a free lunch?"

Kingsley asked as he put the cigarette between his lips.

Daniel pulled it out and tossed it over his shoulder. "If Irina wanted to be paid, I'd pay her."

"I'm not charging for her services. Call it...wear and tear on the bed. You can pay your bill by being in my auction."

"No, thank you."

"Too late. My secretary has already added your name to the program."

"I am not—"

"You are, or I'm telling," Kingsley taunted. Daniel had never punched a Frenchman in the face before, never wanted to. Then again, he'd never fucked a dominatrix before either, so today might be a day of many firsts.

"You said yourself he's a pacifist. What's he going to do? Pray for me to get struck by lightning?"

"He'll keep you from ever seeing her again."

That hit. That hit hard. It hit hard because Daniel believed it.

"Not even talk to her? Really? He's that possessive? That controlling?"

"He'll state the facts—you can't talk to her, and she can't talk to you. The end. *Fin.*"

Daniel already regretted coming back here. The sex had been good, the kink even better, but it was a trap, and he'd stepped right into it.

"Why do you even want me in your stupid auction?"

"You're fresh meat. All us other dominants are old news." Kingsley turned and sat on the sofa in the music room and finally lit his smoke with the flick of a silver lighter. "The girls are already mad about you. You're rich, good-looking, you'll make me a lot of money. I mean, you'll make our *charity* a lot of money. And maybe the other dominant we had dropped out, and we can't find a replacement on short notice."

"Ah, so you don't want me. You need me."

"It's tradition." Kingsley shrugged. "And perhaps you'll meet someone and stop obsessing over a girl you can't have."

"I'm not obsessing."

Kingsley exhaled and stood up again. Daniel tensed as Kingsley came to him. He had a feline sort of slink, like a big cat about to spring for the kill. The kill or the kiss. One never knew with the King of the Underground.

"Where did you go after she left you? Hmm?" Kingsley narrowed his eyes, brought the cigarette to his lips.

"Tierra del Fuego."

"And why did you go there?"

"She and I joked about it."

"You went to the bottom of the world, as close as you can get to Ant-fucking-arctica without going to Ant-fucking-arctica just to send her a postcard as a joke."

"I also wanted to see the condors."

"You need a new girl to obsess over. One who

isn't taken. You'll meet lots of them at the auction. Either do it or don't, but if you don't, well…"

"If I don't, I'll never see her again."

"Irina's right. You are a smart man." Kingsley tapped his temple. "*Très intelligent.*"

Daniel wasn't about to be railroaded, not by a man dressed for a Regency romance novel cover. "I'll be in your stupid auction, but I want to see her. Soon. Just to talk."

Kingsley tick-tocked his head side to side as if considering Daniel's terms. "Fine. I'll arrange it. The auction is in two weeks. In the meantime, get some decent clothes. Please. For my sake and Anya's. And anyone with eyes. We can't have you in the auction looking like that."

He slapped Daniel on the arm and slinked away.

Daniel exhaled heavily. "I never should have left Tierra del Fuego."

———

THE NEXT MORNING, Daniel woke up sore all over. Not from the sex, though he was certain Irina would be a little sore today. Not from old age—he was in the best shape of his life after spending a year climbing mountains. No, he was sore because he'd slept on the couch.

Nice couch, as couches go. Everything was nice in the apartment. On the twenty-sixth floor of the most exclusive high rise in Lenox Hill, the apartment was the finest money could buy: three elegant bedrooms, ten-foot ceilings, hand-crafted molding, built-in cabinets and bookcases, marble countertops, the works. Eleanor might also call his place swanky.

Swanky as it was, Daniel didn't feel at home here anymore. Too big. Too much. Too empty. The air was stale and smelled of disinfectant, the housekeeper having overdone it in preparation for his arrival. It smelled more like a hospital than a home.

Hence the couch. It might not make a good bed, but no one would say it didn't come with a great view.

Daniel rolled over and stared out the floor-to-ceiling window.

The sun was rising high over the East River, and the city was starting to steam.

Hot town, summer in the city... Maggie would always sing that on sizzling July days like this one was going to be. He hated that song, and she loved it. Now he'd kill to hear her sing it again.

It felt like another life, a past life, when he and Maggie had lived here together as Master and slave, and also as husband and wife. They'd spent most of their married life here. Maggie worked in Manhattan until she got sick and they moved out to the Big House, as she called their country house in rural New Hampshire. She wanted to die hearing birds singing, she'd said, not sirens. And she had. Four years ago and this was his first time back in New York. It was too big without her. Even the beds were too big without her.

Daniel closed his eyes, turned over, trying to make himself comfortable enough on the couch to go back to sleep.

No luck. Daniel's phone beeped. What the hell? He'd been back in the city one day, had gotten his new phone yesterday afternoon. How did anyone have the number? He grabbed his cell off the coffee table. Kingsley. Did Daniel want to know how he got the number?

Signore Vitale will see you in an hour. Don't be late.

Daniel didn't reply, although he knew he would go. He'd hardly call Kingsley a friend these days, but they had history. Good history. It was Maggie who'd introduced him to Kingsley and his circle of deviants. The world above knew her as a high-powered attorney. The Underground knew her as one of their pre-eminent submissives. Daniel had had no dominant training at all when they started sleeping together. He'd just known what worked for him...and Maggie on her knees in front of him worked. All the rest of the tricks of the trade, Kingsley had taught him. Kingsley had been a part of their life during their happiest years together. And when she got sick, he was still there, unlike so many people who backed away, as if cancer were contagious.

The day the doctors had told them the verdict —"Two months at home, maybe six months if you stay in the hospital..."—had been the worst day of his life. Even worse than the day she died. He'd never forget those beautiful, tired, gray eyes of Maggie's turning to him and saying, "I'd trade a lifetime in a hospital bed for one night with you in our bed." It had killed him to let her give up the fight. But he'd honored her choice and only let himself cry when she wouldn't see.

So two months it was, then. He'd promised her he'd give her the best two months of her life. Anything she wanted—they could go anywhere, do anything...any wild fantasy she could come up with, he'd make it happen. One night after he'd made love to her—carefully so he wouldn't hurt her, she'd whispered a request in his ear.

"Would you let me call Kingsley?"

For his wife, a month, maybe two, from death, he would have called in the entire US Naval Fleet to service her if that's what she wanted.

"No," he'd told Maggie. "But I'll call him for you."

Daniel called Kingsley. And Kingsley did what he always did—he came. Daniel had worried Kingsley would shrink from Maggie when he saw her. Cancer had ravaged his beautiful wife. Turned her into a waif of ninety-five pounds with hair only just beginning to grow back after one month without chemotherapy. Kingsley hadn't even blinked. He'd been his usual charming, seductive self. And that night at the Big House in their bedroom, Kingsley had done a few things to Maggie that impressed even Daniel.

Kingsley treated Maggie like the most erotic, alluring woman on the face of the earth. Because of that kindness, that night when Kingsley gave Maggie a vacation from her cancer, Daniel would do almost anything for him.

Including, apparently, being in this goddamn auction of his. And going to his goddamn tailor. And staying in the goddamn city for two more weeks, this city that felt both crowded and empty.

Groaning, Daniel swiped at his face and dragged himself off the couch. He dressed—jeans, of course, and a t-shirt, mostly clean, and headed out. First stop, his old barbershop. An hour later, he looked much more like himself. Maggie used to say he looked like a spy in a bad disguise, like a secret assassin doing a poor job of pretending to be a tourist. Especially with his dark blond hair in a sleek crew cut, dark suit and aviator sunglasses. He'd kiss her when she said things like that, then say, *The name's Bondage. James Bondage.*

She'd laugh every time, even though it wasn't that funny. God, he missed being married.

But he felt better, seeing his old self in the mirror again. Next stop—Kingsley's tailor. Kingsley wasn't somebody who could just pick up an Armani suit at an upscale shop in Manhattan and have it fitted. No, Kingsley had to do things his own way—in this case, that meant having an ancient Italian in a three-story walk-up in Greenwich Village hand-sew his custom-made suits.

Signore Vitale greeted Daniel with a few more cheek kisses than was entirely necessary. But Daniel didn't protest. Octogenarian Signore Vitale was adorable, a little elf of a man. Daniel waited in the center of the room in front of a three-way mirror. Somewhere Signore Vitale had a real shop with racks of clothes. But only his most special clients received an invite to his workroom.

"I get my assistant. She has better eyes for the measuring. I'll leave you in her hands." Signore Vitale disappeared behind a curtain, and a woman came out a few minutes later. She wore a 1940s era gray wool suit with flesh-colored stockings and her red hair in a neat knot at the nape of her neck. Daniel barely recognized her at first, as she wore prim reading glasses perched on the end of her nose. Then she spoke.

"Oh...it's you," Anya said, crossing her arms.

"What do you know," Daniel said. "Celine Dion has a day job."

4

"Celine Dion has several jobs," Anya said. "I have five brothers and sisters back home in Montreal to help support."

Anya took out a tiny notebook from her jacket pocket and an even tinier pencil. She flipped to a fresh page, ignoring his eyes on her.

"Five brothers and sisters? Good Lord. Your poor mother."

"Very poor mother." She unfurled a yellow tape measure and slapped it across his back, shoulder to shoulder. "She died five years ago."

Daniel winced in sympathy. While he was mourning his wife, she was mourning her mother. A loss just as painful. She showed no emotion as she stood in front of him to measure the width of his chest.

"And your father?"

Anya rolled her eyes behind her reading glasses. "My father? He sits in pubs all day with other old men, drinking himself to death and planning wars that will never happen to free Quebec from our Canadian overlords. He's forgotten he even has children. Raise your arms."

Daniel lifted both arms. He'd thought Anya had a chip on her shoulder, but no, she was carrying the weight of the world there.

He wanted to hold her. The idea popped into his head first, then the image of her in his arms. He imagined he'd get a pencil to the heart if he tried it. Might be worth it.

Still, the desire lingered, as did the embarrassment that he'd misjudged her so severely. When he'd seen her at Kingsley's, he'd assumed she was nothing but another rich party girl, a socialite's rebellious daughter. Kink was not a poor man's game. Whips and floggers and steel spreader bars with leather cuffs didn't come cheap. But no, she was a hard-working young woman with five siblings she was trying to support. If he'd been reluctant about being part of the auction before, now he was determined to see it through, if only to make sure Anya would be safe.

Just as he started to feel real sympathy for the girl, she nearly strangled him with the measuring tape while checking his neck size.

As she jotted down his numbers, Daniel studied her face. A shame she disliked him so much. He'd rarely seen a more beautiful girl in his life. A straight nose and soft, kissable skin. Long, lush eyelashes and an oval face. If he were an artist, he could spend his life sketching that face in every possible light. But preferably by candlelight. One candle right by the bed and her naked underneath him. Now that would make for a pretty picture.

"You're staring at me." Anya slammed her notebook and pencil onto the table as she picked up her measuring tape again.

"You're beautiful. Of course, I'm staring."

Anya released another disgusted sigh. "You rich dominants...you think women exist for your pleasure alone."

Daniel started to protest, but Anya suddenly dropped to her knees in front of him. He swallowed as his stomach contracted hard. In the mirror, he could see her skirt ride up just enough to catch a flash of garter and pale thigh.

"Spread your legs," she ordered. "And if you say, 'That's my line,' I will shove my pencil into your testicles."

"Never even occurred to me." Daniel obediently spread his legs hip-width apart while Anya unfurled the measuring tape. "So, is this how you met Kingsley? Working for Vitale?"

"Yes." Anya placed the end of the tape at the underside of his crotch. Daniel closed his eyes and thought of the festering bite wound of a Patagonian lancehead viper he'd seen on the leg of a tourist in Argentina. It helped. "He tried to make me measure his inseam twice. I told him I'd use his balls as a pincushion. He hired me on the spot."

Daniel laughed. Typical. "Not many women can resist Kingsley. It must have impressed him that you did."

Anya glared up at him from the floor. "I work sixty hours a week for the Signore. I don't have time to date." She made a note of his left leg measurement.

"Kingsley doesn't date, either. He acquires."

"He won't acquire me. He said I could keep my full share at the auction. He won't even deduct his fifteen percent. The last virgin made two-hundred and fifty thousand dollars."

"Yes, but one of the other women he auctioned off a few years ago got bought by a psycho who choked her so hard she ended up in the hospital." In a perfect world, kink was entirely consensual and nobody ever got hurt more than they wanted to get hurt. This was far from a perfect world.

"Kingsley promised that wouldn't happen to me. And even if I got hurt, it would be worth it. That's enough money to get my brothers and sisters our own place to live. Getting them away from my father is all I care about."

Anya pulled the measuring tape away and stood. Looking down at her notes, she chuckled mischievously, almost flirtatiously.

"What?" Daniel asked.

She raised her eyebrow at him. "Kingsley's inseam...it's an inch longer than yours."

Daniel glared at Anya. "You're in trouble now, Celine."

She giggled nervously. She sounded her age for once, like a young woman enjoying herself.

He stepped toward her using his superior size to corral her into the bend of the three-way mirror. God, he wanted to turn her around, raise the back of her skirt, and fuck that chip right off her shoulder. He'd watch her face in the mirror while inside her, and before he'd let her come, he'd make her say something nice about Canadians.

Him specifically.

Daniel raised a hand to her face. With the tip of his finger, he traced her bottom lip.

He waited for her to bite his finger off. She didn't.

"You should tell me to stop," he said.

"I should? I mean...I should, yes."

He stroked her jawline with the back of his fingers. She shivered. He felt it, saw it. "Are you going to?"

"Soon."

Ah, he knew it. She might hate him, but she also liked him whether she wanted to or not.

He bent his head and put his mouth to her ear. "Have dinner with me tonight."

Anya's skin flushed. She breathed in quick and sharp and then seemingly forgot to breathe out again. A good sign. He looked down at her, blushing and trembling and beautiful beyond belief.

"I have to work. Kingsley wants a new suit for the auction, and now I have to start on your wardrobe. You can afford the time and money to eat dinner. I can't." She sounded unsure, as if she were trying to talk herself out of it.

"I'm buying. I'll take you anywhere you want, buy you anything you want."

It was the wrong thing to say. Her eyes flashed, and she stepped to the side, escaping him. She turned her back to him and jotted down more numbers in her notebook.

The spell was broken.

"You go buy your own dinner. I'm not on the menu."

———

DANIEL LEFT Signore Vitale's and headed to Kingsley's. They needed to talk. Specifically, they needed to talk about Anya. Somewhere past the facade of the wicked King of the Underworld, Kingsley had a heart. It was hidden and hidden deep, but Daniel was sure it was there. He'd seen a glimpse of it the night Kingsley had come to see Maggie before she died. If Daniel could find that heart again, maybe he could talk Kingsley into taking Anya out of this stupid auction. This wasn't fun and it wasn't funny. She was selling herself to the city's most hardened deviants—Daniel knew many of them personally—to take care of her five younger siblings. There had to be a better way to help her. A way that didn't make him picture a lamb wandering blindly into the path of a wolf.

And once that discussion ended, they might discuss Daniel's participation in this idiotic auction and how it wasn't going to happen until he got to see Eleanor.

Daniel didn't bother going to the front door this time. Instead, he had the cab drop him off at the side entrance, which led to the back stairs of the old servants' quarters. Most of the Underground didn't even know the townhouse had a side entrance. As a handful of Kingsley's clients weren't just rich but also famous, they needed a way to sneak in and out of the house anonymously.

Daniel climbed the back stairs and found Kingsley in the hallway outside a door engaged in a profoundly passionate kiss with a dark-skinned goddess almost as tall as Kingsley himself. Kingsley apparently noticed Daniel waiting. Somehow, he managed to give Daniel a questioning look and slip the goddess a little more tongue at the same time.

The goddess finally pulled away and disappeared into Kingsley's bedroom.

"Your timing is impeccable, *mon ami*." Kingsley straightened his crushed cravat.

"Sorry for the interruption," Daniel said without a trace of actual contrition.

"I'm not. The girl's insatiable. I'm French. Not a machine."

"She's gorgeous."

Kingsley nodded. "Tahitian. The newest member of—"

"Yes, the Imperial Collection. Right. That's why I'm here."

"You know my Collection is like your library." Kingsley led them toward the back staircase. "You are welcome to check anything out as long as you return it in time."

Daniel's stomach dropped a few inches at his joke. Of course Kingsley didn't know how close those words hit to home. Suddenly that day in the library after his first night with Eleanor came back to him with crystal clarity.

So you are a librarian. What does that make me then? A seven-day loan? Eleanor had asked, flashing her eyes at him. And then she laughed. That laugh like a champagne cork popping. He still heard that laugh in his dreams.

"I don't want to borrow anyone from your collection. I want to talk about Anya."

"Really? What about Anya?"

"Don't say it like that."

"Like what?" Kingsley shrugged innocently, oh-so-innocently.

"You could have warned me she worked for Vitale."

"Did you need to be warned? She's a pretty girl who doesn't like you, not a criminal."

"What game are you playing here?"

"One where nobody loses," Kingsley said. "So what's the harm?"

"The harm is Anya getting hurt. Did you know

she has five brothers and sisters she's trying to rescue from her father?"

"I knew she came from a big family. She never told me she was afraid for her family. Interesting she confided in you and not me. Isn't it?"

It was a little interesting, but Daniel didn't have time to analyze her motivations. "I don't want her in this auction. Find someone else to be your token virgin."

"That's her decision, not mine or yours," Kingsley said. "She volunteered. No one forced her. And I warned her several times that what she was signing up for might not be worth the money."

"I'll give her some money. As much as she needs."

"You think she'd take it from you?"

"No, but you can say it's from you."

"She won't take it from me, either. She won't take charity. I've offered. Too much pride."

"Why are you so determined to ruin her life?"

"Why are you so determined to *run* her life?"

Daniel was silenced. Kingsley had a way of punching one in the stomach without lifting a finger. He could do it with a single question.

Why was he so determined to run her life? He barely knew her.

"I know you're trying to be a good man," Kingsley said. "You've always been a good man. Too good for the likes of us around here. I knew that the day Maggie brought you to us, that you would never quite fit in. Your halo would keep getting caught on our pitchforks."

A small smile crossed Daniel's lips—quickly, then was gone just as quickly.

"You have a hero's heart," Kingsley said. "And you're always looking for someone to rescue. You rescued Maggie from loneliness and now you're hooked on rescuing women, like it's a drug. You tried to rescue Eleanor from him. You saw how that worked out? Hmm? Now you want to rescue Anya, and I don't remember hearing her asking anyone for help."

Daniel glanced at the ground.

"Just because someone needs help, doesn't give you the right to force them to take it," Kingsley continued. "And if there's one sin in this house— it's forcing someone to do something against their will. The second Anya asks to be let out of the auction, she'll be out. And if she doesn't, she's in. And if she won't say it to you, I will—mind your own business. *Tu comprend*?"

With extreme reluctance, Daniel replied, "*Je comprends.*"

"Good man. Come on. I'll walk you out."

They started down the stairs, but when they hit the first landing, Daniel stiffened in shock. A sound he hadn't heard in a year and a half echoed up to them.

But not just any sound.

A laugh.

A laugh like the popping of a champagne cork.

Daniel froze and met Kingsley's dark, watching eyes.

"Eleanor's here?" Daniel whispered.

Kingsley didn't answer at first. The charming French rogue had disappeared again and the dangerous guardian of the Underground gave him a steely warning stare.

"Non, *mon ami*," he finally answered. "*They* are here."

5

Daniel didn't move, couldn't move. And as long as Kingsley stood there watching him, he wouldn't move. But he listened. He heard a man's voice, low and stern, a voice he hadn't heard since that one perfect week with Eleanor. Then he heard her laugh again. That laugh, so joyous and lusty...it floated up the stairs and passed through him, chilling him to the core.

The voices retreated and Kingsley raised his hand, beckoning Daniel to follow him in silence. At the next landing, they stopped and waited. From their post, he and Kingsley could stay hidden in the shadows and still look into the private drawing room at the back of the townhouse.

There she was. The girl he'd been thinking of non-stop, even while inside other women, for the past year and a half.

Eleanor...she looked as beautiful now as the day he first saw her. She wore a white summer dress that showed off her legs, her black hair was pulled high on her head in a messy knot, and around her graceful neck was her white collar. At the liquor cabinet, she poured two glasses of white wine, then carried them back to a table where she offered one— with a curtsy—to a tall blond man in black trousers, black jacket, and a white shirt open at the collar.

Him. Søren.

Daniel watched as Eleanor sat opposite Søren at a small game table, a chessboard between them. They spoke in low tones. Daniel couldn't hear what was said, but it made her smile.

Even cowering in the shadows on the staircase landing, looking far down into the sitting room, Daniel could see the radiant happiness shining in her eyes as she feigned luxurious, yawning boredom. Søren casually reached out and snapped his fingers in her face to get her attention. Instantly sat up straighter. With reluctance, Daniel dragged his eyes from her to gaze at Søren, a man he once considered a friend but now, since losing her, thought of as a rival. He hated himself for the bitterness he harbored in his heart toward Eleanor's owner. But no amount of reasoning and rationalizing could help him swallow the bitter pill that remained lodged in his throat since the moment he'd asked her to stay with him and she'd said, "No."

"He's a priest," Daniel said in a voice so soft he doubted Kingsley heard.

"He is."

"How can she be that happy with him?"

Looking at her face, her eyes, he had no doubt he was looking at a woman completely and utterly in love. "He can't marry her. Can't give her children... not without getting excommunicated."

"She doesn't want marriage. She doesn't want children."

"What does she want?"

"Him," Kingsley said simply. His laugh was the low rumble of a distant train. "Trust me, my friend, there's no way to break them up. Even I know they belong together."

Daniel heard something in Kingsley's voice, a note of bitterness that matched his own. Together they stared at the couple in the drawing room—the tall man in all black—handsome, distinguished, intimidating.

And her—that wild black hair, those black and green eyes, those full lips...lips designed for acts more intimate than simply kissing other lips.

Daniel noted that while his own eyes studied every line and curve of Eleanor, Kingsley's gaze focused elsewhere, onto the face of the man who owned her, onto the face of Kingsley's best, and some would say only, friend.

The sight of them together, so content, briefly overwhelmed him. Closing his eyes, Daniel found himself hurtled into the past, further than he wanted to go.

Back to the day of his wife's funeral.

How he'd even gotten dressed that morning

remained a mystery. He'd been able to knot his tie but only from muscle memory.

"I'm burying my wife today," was the refrain that echoed through his mind. "I'm a widower at thirty-four...and I don't know why."

He must have spoken the words aloud because he heard an answer from the door to his and Maggie's bedroom.

"I'm certain it will be of no consolation to you, but I don't know why either."

Daniel turned and there stood a six-foot-four blond priest. Søren.

"Actually, it is a consolation. I don't want to live in a world where Maggie's death makes sense."

Søren studied Daniel with kind, searching eyes. Kingsley had come by earlier with a gift from his medicine cabinet, and the combination of the tranquilizer and the shock were the only two forces keeping Daniel vertical.

"I won't insult you by asking you how you are. I will only ask you what I can do to help you today."

Daniel remembered the rush of gratitude, knowing that he didn't have to dissemble. He could tell Søren anything, confess any secret and it would be absolved.

"If I asked you to kill me, would you?"

The priest smiled. "No, though I won't judge you for wanting to die. I would, too, in your shoes."

That helped. It helped that this man who seemed to know all the answers to all the questions that had ever been or would ever be asked...it helped to know that he, too, would want to die if he lost his wife. Except he was a Catholic priest and so would never have a wife. Daniel felt almost sorry for the man.

"Perhaps there's something else? Something other than a mercy killing?"

"Yes. Maybe. I don't think I could stand it..." Daniel paused and tried to put his words in order. "If anyone touches me today or talks to me, I won't make it. And I have to get through this. For her."

Søren clasped his hands in front of him at the wrist. Daniel didn't recall ever seeing the Priest of the Underground in his long medieval-looking cassock before. Usually, he was in layman's clothes at Kingsley's house—jeans and a white button-down shirt and jacket, or black pants and black t-shirt. In the floor-length black cassock with the tie around the waist, Søren appeared even more intimidating than usual, like a being from an ancient world.

"You want me to keep everyone away from you then?" Søren asked.

Again Daniel nodded. Or tried to. His body and mind seemed to be working independently of each other.

"That I can do for you."

For the next two hours, Daniel stared straight ahead—he heard nothing, saw no one but for a blur of black behind him hovering like a dark angel. If anyone came to speak to Daniel, Søren would raise his hand to stop them, then he'd lower his head and whisper into their ear. What he said, Daniel didn't hear. But it worked. Everyone nodded, turned, walked away.

Only at the graveside did Daniel come back to awareness again. He stood staring down at the coffin as friends and family made their way back to their cars. Even the minister and his own parents finally gave up waiting on him and walked away. Only his dark angel remained—not speaking, not consoling, merely present.

"My wife is in a box in the ground," he said more to himself than Søren. "I should be in it with her."

A long silence stood between them. Daniel sensed the priest weighing his words.

"Only Kingsley knows this," the priest began, "but I now have someone in my life. Her name is Eleanor."

"Pretty name."

"If something ever happened to my Eleanor..." He paused and took a breath. "There would be no hole, no chasm, no canyon deep enough to contain my grief."

No hole...no chasm...no canyon deep enough... Daniel felt the truth, the rightness of those words in his soul.

"I'm lost." His unblinking eyes began to water. "I don't know what to do."

"What do you want to do?"

"Sleep. For years maybe. Hibernate. Dig a hole

in the ground and bury myself until I can face the world without her."

"Then do that."

Daniel turned his head and met the priest's eyes—eyes the color and strength of steel. "What if I can't ever get out of that hole again?"

"Do you trust me, Daniel?"

Did he trust Søren? Daniel had friends, loads of them. He had a sister he loved and in-laws who treated him like their own. He still had lunch once a month with the professor who had mentored him in school. If anyone asked who his best friend was, he would have said his eighty-year-old grandfather.

But the day he found out Maggie had cancer, it was Søren he called. Søren, a Jesuit priest fluent in over a dozen languages, the beloved pastor of a small but devoted congregation, and the wisest, most erudite man Daniel had ever met.

And when Daniel told him about Maggie, Søren said exactly the right thing.

"Fuck."

If that was all a priest—a priest who could rattle off entire books of the Bible from memory— if that was all he could find to say, then it was all there was to say.

Daniel had laughed and then he'd cried. He knew he'd called the right man.

When Daniel finally answered Søren, he spoke with complete sincerity.

"Yes, I trust you."

"Then go home," he said. "Bury yourself in your hole in the ground if you need to. If you can't find your way out again, we'll send someone to dig you out."

And for three years he hadn't been able to dig his way out of the hole of grief he'd fallen into. For three years, he didn't set one foot off their Big House property. But Søren had kept his promise. He sent his own property to him, his own Eleanor, his own heart.

But that was the past.

Now in the present, he watched Eleanor in the drawing room. She held a chess piece in her hand. Søren pointed to a square on the board, but she shook her head. Knowing him, he was attempting to teach her the finer points of some obscure strategy. Knowing her, she was playing by suicide rules, trying to lose on purpose to end the game quicker. Again Søren snapped his fingers in her face. Again she shook her head. Daniel heard him release an exasperated sigh. He reached for the chess piece but she popped it into her mouth.

"*Merde*...not again..." Kingsley sighed.

Daniel only watched as Søren reached out and pinched her nose closed. The battle of wills began. With her mouth closed and her nose pinched, Eleanor had no hope of winning this fight. The need to breathe would eventually overcome her willful refusal to play the game by His rules.

A minute passed. Eleanor clenched her eyes shut. Søren held out his hand, tapped under her chin, and she gave in and spit the piece into his palm.

"*Merci mon Dieu*," Kingsley breathed.

"What?"

Kingsley looked at Daniel. "Last time she swallowed it."

"By accident?" Daniel winced. That couldn't have been pleasant—going down or coming out.

"On purpose."

Daniel raised his hand and covered his mouth to stifle his laugh.

In the drawing room, Eleanor turned her face toward the shadows on the landing. Daniel took a step back deeper in the darkness.

Kingsley beckoned him back upstairs and Daniel wrenched his eyes from Eleanor. If she saw him...if Søren saw him, it wouldn't be good. Maybe, eventually, he could see Eleanor without wanting to drag her to him and beat and fuck the memory of any other man out of her head. Maybe someday...but not today.

At the top of the stairs, Daniel turned his back to Kingsley just long enough to catch his breath.

"Can I get you anything?" Kingsley prompted. "Perhaps a member of my Imperial Collection could take your mind off her?"

Daniel turned, grabbed Kingsley by the throat and shoved him hard and fast into the wall.

"I'm not in a great mood right now so you'll just have to forgive me," Daniel nearly growled the words. "One of these days you're actually going to care about a woman instead of collecting them like stamps in your passport. If Anya ends up getting hurt because of this stupid fucking sex auction of yours, I'll show you and the priest downstairs what real sadism looks like. *Tu comprend?*"

Kingsley stared him down. Daniel knew that for all his devil-may-care airs, Kingsley might easily qualify as one of the more dangerous men in the city, if not the country. But when Daniel looked into his eyes, he saw the tiniest shred of fear. Daniel grinned.

"*Je comprends*," Kingsley said.

"Good."

Daniel relinquished his hold on Kingsley's neck and stepped back.

Once more Kingsley had cause to straighten his crumpled collar.

"Now I'm leaving," Daniel said and headed toward the front stairs. "I'm going to go have dinner. I'm going to go to my apartment. And I'm not going to think about you or Eleanor or him or this world you've sucked me back into."

Kingsley raised his eyebrow at him. "If I recall, it is you who knocked on my door, Daniel."

"Yes, and once this auction is over, I'll never knock on it again. I'll stick around long enough to make sure Anya survives this without getting hurt. Then I'm gone."

Daniel started down the hall.

"It was a test, *mon ami*."

Even as he spun around to face Kingsley, Daniel regretted the decision. "What was a test?"

"That week together—you and her. It was a test."

Daniel glared back, and Kingsley laughed his infuriating French laugh.

Kingsley strolled toward him. "Lest you think he sent her to you out of some great affection for you...let me explain, it was a test."

"Let me guess—I failed."

"You were not the one being tested, Daniel. She was. And she passed."

The cold truth of the statement hit Daniel hard in the stomach and harder even lower. He wanted to answer, wanted to say something, to deny it. But he had no words. She could have had him— someone rich, someone single, someone free. She could have had someone who could have married her, given her children, a life in the open...and yet she'd walked away from it all and chosen Søren instead. Instead of a wife, she was the mistress of priest. Instead of children, she had secrets. Instead of Daniel, she had Søren.

Daniel closed his eyes. Not even a masochist would have enjoyed this kind of pain. Daniel took one second to imagine punching Kingsley's handsome face into an unrecognizable pulp. It made him feel better. A little.

"Let her go," Kingsley said, and his voice was almost, but not quite, kind. "She's not for you. She never was. You're in love with a fantasy, a girl you can save from a sadist who will never marry her or give her children. That girl doesn't exist." He put his hand on Daniel's shoulder. "Maggie loved you and would want you to find love again. That way," he said, nodding his head toward the darkened stairs, toward Eleanor, "is not where you'll find it."

———

DANIEL SAID NOTHING. He stared at the dark stairway, wanting to go down it, to call Eleanor's name, to hear the truth from her own lips. Until he did, he wouldn't believe it.

He didn't. And he didn't wait for Kingsley to speak again, either. Daniel left by the main stairs. He went out the front door and hailed the first cab he saw. It took him home, but only long enough for him to change clothes. Then he went for a run, a long, hard run through Central Park. The heat was nearly unbearable. It felt like running in a sauna, but he craved the mindlessness, the release of endorphins, the punishment.

But he couldn't outrun memories of her.

He remembered the night he and Eleanor had played a game of strip poker. He played to win. She played to lose. After three hands, she was down to her white lacy panties. He dealt another hand.

"Hit me," she'd said, rolling onto her stomach, her bare legs in the air and nothing on her from the waist up but a smile.

"This is poker," he reminded her.

Every evening was spent in the living room by his fireplace talking, fucking, sometimes both at the same time.

"Poker? I don't even know her."

Daniel reached out and flicked the end of her nose. "Behave yourself."

"Never." She threw a few cards down. "Hit me."

"Poker," he repeated. "Not blackjack."

Eleanor looked up at him through the veil of her wavy black hair. "Maybe I'm not talking about the game."

Daniel nearly dropped the cards. "You do realize we've only known each other for a few days," he reminded her.

She shrugged her shoulders, her soft, pale shoulders he'd bruised with bites and rough kisses just a few hours earlier, though the hunger to bruise her with a flogger was growing.

"You've fucked me more times than I can count, ordered me around, made me call you 'sir'... but still you haven't hit me. You know you want to...*sir.*"

She flipped onto her back and looked up at him. Was there anything in the world more beautiful than a woman's naked breasts bathed in the light of a fireplace? Especially Eleanor's breasts by his fireplace?

"I take inflicting pain very seriously," he'd said even though everything in him ached to tie her to his bed and paint her pale skin bright red with welts. "That's a lot of trust. Do you really trust me that much? After only a few days?"

"No, I don't. But I trust him. And he trusts you. After all, I'm not submitting to you this week. I'm submitting to him."

"Answer this question—how long did you know him before he beat you the first time?" Daniel asked.

Eleanor groaned melodramatically.

"Yes, I forgot," he said. "You don't want to talk about him."

She nodded as she sat up.

"Can you at least answer me in sign language?"

Eleanor reached out and took the deck of cards from him. She flipped through the cards and found the Five of Clubs.

"Five years?" Daniel asked and she nodded again. "Five years. Not a few days," he said pointedly. "So he waited five years not only to hit you, but to have sex with you. And you're ready for that with me after a few days?"

She nodded eagerly.

Daniel looked down at the cards scattered about. "Are you really happy with him?" he asked, not quite sure where that question came from.

She sighed heavily as if she'd been asked and had answered that question a thousand times before. "Everyone thinks because he's so quiet and serious..."

"And a sadist," he reminded her.

"Everyone thinks he's this." She held up the

King of Clubs who grasped a sword in each hand. "But he isn't. Not with me. With me he's..."

She dug through all the cards until she had a full suit.

On the floor between them she arranged the cards.

All hearts.

"And who are you?" Daniel swallowed hard, her devotion to her owner a painful reminder of how close he and Maggie had been. Would he ever have that again? "Her?"

He picked up the Queen of Hearts.

"Oh, no." She reached past him and grabbed the card box. "This is me."

She held up the Joker.

"Is that because you're funny or because you're Gotham's worst nightmare?"

"That's for me to know and you to find out. In the meantime, how about a little game of..."

She picked up two cards. One a Six of Clubs, the other a Nine of Spades.

Daniel glared at her. "Now I *am* going to beat you."

He hadn't been joking. He grabbed her wrist and dragged her to her feet. In less than a minute, he had her in the bedroom with her back pressed to the bedpost. He devoured her mouth, her soft lips even as his fingers dug into her hips. With a ruthless shove he pushed her onto the floor. He didn't even have to give her the order. She opened his pants and took him deep in her mouth.

He and Maggie had been lovers for a month before he let himself slap her during sex. But her reaction had been so intensely erotic that the very next day he'd invested in an arsenal of S&M gear, an arsenal of S&M gear that had touched no one's skin but Maggie's. For the first time since her death, he would use it on someone else.

Before he came, he pulled away and dragged Eleanor up to her feet again. He threw open a cabinet in his bedroom where he and Maggie stored the gear and took out a flogger, bondage cuffs, and snap hooks. He returned to the bed, wrenched Eleanor's wrists behind her back and buckled the cuffs on.

"Tell me your safe word," he demanded.

"Doesn't matter," she said and he felt her body go slack as she surrendered herself into his hands. "You won't hear it."

He'd almost laughed out loud then. "That tough, are you?"

"No, sir. That well-trained."

And God, she had been. Eleanor stood still, kept her body loose and slack and breathed through the pain like a pro. Of course, the mild beating he inflicted on her probably paled in comparison to what her owner did to her. But her willing submission to the pain, to him, the trust she showed letting him bind her to the bedpost...

After, he'd dropped the flogger, pressed his chest to her back, pushed into her hard and deep. Her wetness and heat enveloped him. Before

Eleanor came to him, he'd been celibate for three long and lonely years. That night he was determined to make up for lost time.

Right before coming he wrenched himself away from her, picked up the flogger and beat her again. Harder this time, hard enough she finally let out a real grunt of pain. And that sound hit him harder than his flogger hit her. Again he thrust into her and as he thrust, he felt himself clawing his way out of the ground, the dirt falling away, the fresh air of the wide world filling his lungs. With every brutal movement he came more back to life, more back to himself again.

Finally, he released her from her bonds and dragged her to the floor. In an instant he was on her and in her.

After he came, he tried crawling off her, found he didn't have the energy, and merely collapsed onto her prone body. He started to apologize for going too far, for losing control. But once again he heard that laugh. That incredibly erotic laugh. Homer, he decided then and there, had gotten all it wrong. The sirens of ancient lore were singers. The real siren's song was a laugh.

"What?" he'd asked, kissing the back of her shoulder.

"Now that," she said, stretching out underneath him, seemingly fully content to let him stay inside her all night, "was poker."

He'd laughed. This girl even made bad puns during sex.

Daniel couldn't run anymore.

He jogged to a water fountain and drank himself sick. Then he splashed water on his face and ran it through his hair. After, he was too wet and sweaty for a taxi so he walked back to his building in Lenox Hill. He'd strip naked the second he got home. Take a shower, pour a whiskey, drink himself into a stupor. Tomorrow—lather, rinse, repeat.

Stalking through his apartment, he pulled his shirt off on the way to his bedroom. In the doorway he paused when he found a naked girl kneeling with her back to him on his bed.

Long black hair, voluptuous body... Now where had he seen that before?

"Irina—how did you get in here?" he asked, surprised but not entirely displeased to see his beautiful Russian again.

The girl turned her head and gave him a wicked grin. "Did you miss me?"

"God. Eleanor."

aniel could barely breathe from the shock. Eleanor...naked...kneeling on his bed and grinning at him like the last eighteen months had been the setup to a bad joke, and finally, here she was to deliver the punchline.

"Nope, just me. God's out today."

Daniel took nearly ten whole seconds to process Eleanor's words, but it only took one second to get to her. He slid across the bed and took her into his arms.

"You...what are you doing here?" He held her tight to his chest, stroked her hair, her back.

"You sent me a postcard from Tierra del Fuego. The least I could do is stop in and say, 'Hello.'"

Daniel took her face in his hands. Her eyes shone black as night and her body molded into his.

"Hello." Then he took ownership of her mouth with a kiss so ferocious he knew her lips would be swollen for a day from it. He didn't care. If this is how she returned the favor of a single postcard... he wished he'd sent her a thousand of them.

His hands roamed her body, sliding down her back, grasping her bottom, digging deep into her soft skin. The kiss she returned with equal ferocity as she reached between their bodies to open his pants.

"Are you sure?" he asked, afraid of her answer.

"I'm naked on your bed. Did you think I stopped by for a game of blackjack?"

"The game is poker."

Eleanor laughed, and her laughter filled the room, the apartment, the building, the whole city, and even his heart that for so long had sat empty.

Weaving his fingers through her hair, he kissed her again. And again. He couldn't get enough of her mouth, the taste of her lips, the tease of her tongue against his.

"I can't believe you're here," he breathed into her ear, and, while there, bit her earlobe.

"I heard your laugh on the stairs. I don't know how, but I knew it was you."

"King wouldn't have given you my address."

Eleanor laughed again, low, throaty, and playfully sinister. "I beat it out of him."

"What about—" *Søren*, he tried to say, but she cut him off.

"Are you going to keep giving me the third degree, sir? Or are you going to beat me and fuck me like your life depends on it?"

Breathing in, he inhaled her scent—lilies, orchids—the subtle essence of every hothouse flower he could name graced her skin. She'd always seemed like a hothouse flower—something beautiful and wild, yet thrived best in captivity.

If only he could keep her. "My life does depend on it."

"Well, then..." She slid her hands over his bare shoulders and met his eyes. "Maybe we should stop wasting time."

She pushed his running shorts down and took his hard cock in her hands. Burying his mouth in the crook of her neck, he groaned as the hands he'd dreamed of for a year and a half did everything he remembered they could. With her slim, nimble fingers, she traced the length and width of him, gently caressed the sensitive underside, and cupped his testicles. He groaned with the shameless abandon of a submissive.

"You have to stop, or I'll come in your hands," he warned her.

"Oh, no. Not that. Anything but that." Eleanor pushed him onto his back, and he went willingly. She wrenched his shorts off and threw them against the wall with the flourish of a matador. Then she pushed his legs apart and kissed the inside of his ankle. She kissed the soft indentation right under his quad muscles before dipping her head and biting his inner thigh—hard. Daniel winced. Eleanor only laughed.

Daniel's head fell back as she wrapped her lips around his cock and caressed it with her tongue.

With torturously light licks and kisses, she focused her attention solely on the head. As erotic as it was, he needed more than just pleasure. He craved connection. He reached down and found her hand, twined their fingers together.

Real...she was real and warm and here, and God, she was sucking his cock like she missed him as much as he missed her. He knew he'd be fooling himself to believe that. She'd picked Søren over him, and she would probably do it again. Why she was here now, he didn't know, and he didn't care. All he could do was let go and enjoy it.

He let go. With a soft cry and spurt after spurt of come, he filled her mouth. Her throat moved as she swallowed every drop he gave her.

When it was done, Eleanor sat up on her knees and licked her lips. Daniel took her in his arms and pulled her onto him, laying her against his chest.

"I still can't believe you're here."

"I'm here." She smiled blissfully, a little drunkenly. "For now."

"Kingsley said if I agreed to be in his stupid auction, he'd let me see you again."

"You got conned. King doesn't get to decide who I see and don't see."

"But Søren does."

"If you really believe that, you don't know me very well."

Daniel laughed softly. "Here I thought you

were the world's greatest submissive. Turns out, you're the world's greatest actress."

"I really am a terrible submissive. I submit when I want to, not when he wants me to. Which is fine with him. According to him, it's more fun to punish me when I deserve it."

"You always deserve it."

She turned her face up to his, grinned, and Daniel kissed her, tasting himself on her lips. The mix of his salt and her sweetness set his blood to boiling again. Pushing her onto her back, he pinned her wrists to the bed.

"I know you'll go back to him tonight." Daniel dipped his head and lightly sucked on each nipple before kissing his way back to the hollow of her throat, "but you'll take my bruises with you."

Helpless underneath him, she panted. "Yes, sir."

He dragged her from the bed by her wrists and left her standing at the footboard.

"Kneel," he ordered, and she went down onto her knees.

He drank in the sight of her, of this woman he'd longed for day and night for so long. She knelt at the foot of his bed, her back a blank canvas waiting to be painted with welts. From under the bed, he pulled a large case like the ones Kingsley kept in all his townhouse bedrooms.

"Hands on the top rail."

Eleanor reached up and grasped the top of the metal footboard.

Daniel stood behind her as he handcuffed her wrists to the railing.

"I have very fond memories of this bed," he told her as he pushed her hair off her back. "Maggie and I bought it together. She made sure to lay down and test the strength of the footboard and the headboard. The elderly furniture dealer was slightly horrified."

"I wish I'd known Maggie, sir."

"You remind me of her in so many ways." Daniel knelt behind her and kissed the back of her neck and her shoulders. He ran his hand down her side and across her stomach.

Only when he said the words did he realize how true they were. Eleanor's spirit, her sense of humor, her wild streak that gave him such pleasure to try to tame...so much like Maggie.

"I'll take that as the compliment I know it is, sir."

Daniel didn't answer. Instead, he pressed his lips to the center of her back, kissing the elegant curve of her spine.

He turned his head and bit her, hard, in the center of her back.

She flinched and released a gasp of pain.

"Just marking my target," he whispered in her ear before standing up and grabbing a stiff riding crop from the case.

He counted in his head a full sixty seconds before striking her the first time. She flinched, and the metal of the handcuffs rattled against the metal of the footboard. Music to his ears.

A welt six inches long and the color of fire burned across her pale skin. He struck her again, then again. A fourth time, then a fifth...At ten, she finally broke and cried out. At twelve, he stopped.

He dropped to his knees behind her and pressed his chest to her burning back.

"Did you enjoy that?" he said into her hair.

"Hurt like hell. I loved it."

He reached up and unlocked the cuffs. He knew she'd have to leave sooner or later, and he didn't want to waste a single second with her.

He lifted her off the floor and carried her to the bed. Just to hear that laugh again, he tossed her unceremoniously across the covers. As she was laughing, he grasped her ankles and dragged her hips to the edge of the bed.

No more laughing now.

He went down on his knees for her, spreading her thighs wide and opening her with his fingers. His lips sought her clitoris, and he sucked lightly on it. Her back arched. She pressed harder into his mouth. No woman he'd ever been with tasted quite like her...so sweet and tart at the same time, the scent of her more potent than any drug.

She moaned as he pushed his tongue into her. For the rest of his life, he'd remember the feel of her heels digging into his back and the warmth of her thighs against his face. Still, he couldn't wait any longer. He had to be inside her.

Daniel stood up and lifted her legs over his shoulders as he pushed into her. He wanted to go slow, to savor every second of her. But he couldn't hold back. He thrust into her, hard and deep, savoring the sound of her cry of pleasure.

Eleanor stretched her arms out to each side, and her head fell back in a posture of utter surrender. Daniel slid his hand up her body and took her gently by the throat. Her pulse beat hard under his fingers as he thrust into her again and again.

His fingertips found her clitoris and gently teased it. She responded just as he knew she would, as he remembered she would, grasping at the sheets with desperate fingers, hips lifting, her whole body going stiff for a brief eternity before her inner muscles began to spasm, clamping so hard around him they nearly pushed him out of her.

As Eleanor relaxed under him, Daniel only thrust harder, deeper. He held off as long as he could, not wanting to let go of this moment. She was his, if only for now. She was his, if only while she was under him. He wanted to mark her, write "MINE" all over her body. Since he couldn't, he did the next best thing. He pulled out of her and straddled her hips with his knees. When their eyes locked, he finally came on her stomach.

As the tension slowly drained out of him, Daniel collapsed on top of Eleanor and gathered her to him. He sighed and closed his eyes as she lightly scratched his back. The simple mindless gesture of affection so painfully reminiscent of lovemaking with Maggie nearly did him in. He squeezed his eyes shut tighter and tried to imprint this perfect moment into his mind forever.

"Yes," he said, answering the question she asked an hour ago. "I missed you."

———

THEY LAY THERE A LONG TIME, not speaking, only touching.

"Are you going to fall asleep on me?" she asked, tracing his ribcage with her fingers.

"No. I'm just afraid if I open my eyes, I'll wake up and this will all have been a dream."

"If I'm involved, there's a decent chance it's a nightmare. You might want to wake up."

Daniel shook his head and slowly opened his eyes. "The only nightmares you're in are the ones when I wake up and you're still gone."

Eleanor sighed heavily, and Daniel finally rolled off of her. Pulling back the sheets, she scrambled under the covers. He joined her in his bed. He could think of at least three body parts he'd happily sacrifice to be able to find her in his bed every night of his life.

Daniel lay on his back and Eleanor draped herself across his chest.

"You know I inherited a lot of money from Maggie, right?" Daniel asked. "She was loaded and left every penny to me."

"I've seen your country house, remember? And this apartment is bigger than the house I grew up in."

"We could leave, if you wanted. I'd take you anywhere. You'd never have to work a day in your life again. You could—"

"Leave him?" she asked and looked up at Daniel. "No, I can't. Or I can, but I don't want to."

"You say that, but still, you're here—"

"I'm here because we had a great week together, Daniel. And I missed you, and Kingsley said you were still hung up on me." She sat up and pulled her knees to her chest. "But it was one week. Just seven days."

"You're a Catholic, right?" He rolled onto his side and propped his head on his hand. "Don't you think the entire universe was created in seven days?"

"If you haven't noticed already," she said, giving him a pointed look, "I'm a very bad Catholic."

Daniel laughed and caressed her naked leg. "Do you really love him?"

"Of course I do. He's my everything."

"Everything?"

"Lover, owner, priest, best friend?"

"I find that last one hard to believe."

"Because you don't know him the way I do."

Except Daniel did know him the way she did. They had been friends once. Yes, he could believe

Søren was her best friend. He could believe it. He just didn't want to admit it.

"But," she continued, "don't tell anybody I said that. Kingsley likes Blondie to keep his big bad priest rep intact. Admittedly, he is six-four and a sadist, so he is a little intimidating. If you're not me."

"You call Søren 'Blondie'?"

Eleanor grinned. "Of course. Just not to his face. Well...not very often."

Daniel laughed because only laughing would keep him from grabbing her, holding her down, and keeping her there until she wanted him as much as he wanted her.

"It's not fair, you know," Daniel said. "I could give you so much more than he could—"

"Daniel, let me ask you something. Are you going to spend the rest of your life living in the past?"

Her question surprised him enough that he rolled up and leaned back against the headboard to face her. "I'm not. Not anymore. Look...if he died, what would you do?"

Eleanor pursed her lips and hummed. "In this scenario, has he died of natural causes, or did I finally break down and murder him in his sleep? Either is equally likely."

"Natural causes."

Slowly, Eleanor inhaled and exhaled. For once, she seemed to be taking the conversation seriously.

She grabbed a pillow and pulled it to her, clutching it as if for comfort.

"I would die, too. Not physically. But there's no way this Eleanor could go on without him."

"Is there another Eleanor?"

She smiled and nodded. "Horrifying thought, I know. I guess to survive, I'd just think of my life in terms of acts in plays or something. Like how the old movies were so long, they used to have intermissions. Eleanor...Part One, I guess, she would die with him. But Eleanor Part Two would wait for the curtain to go up and she'd step out on the stage and put on one hell of a show. You can't let the curtain stay down before the second act."

Eleanor leaned forward and dragged a hand through his hair. "Maggie's dead. She's been dead for over four years. And I remind you of her and that's why you wanted me so much. Maggie's dead and Daniel Part One is dead. Maybe you let *her* go. I don't know. But I know you haven't let *him* go. Maybe it's time for Daniel Part Two to step out on the stage."

He felt her words in his heart; they hurt more than his crop on her back had hurt her. And as the truth always hurt, he knew her words were true.

"I don't know who he is." Daniel half-whispered the confession.

"Daniel Part Two is everything Daniel Part One was. But wiser, smarter, and even sexier. Seriously, what have you been doing for the past year? You're so cut, I could slice myself open on your quads."

Daniel laughed, almost blushing at her erotic appreciation of his body. "Mountain climbing... trekking through rain forests...stomping all over South America."

"Sounds like hell on earth."

"I loved it."

She shuddered in feigned horror. So much for all his fantasies about her being his traveling companion on his wilderness sojourns.

"So tell me, what did you love most about being Daniel Part One? And don't say anything that has anything to do with camping."

Grinning, Daniel contemplated the question. Not that he really needed to think about it. He knew the answer immediately.

"Maggie. No question."

"Because she was your sub? Your property?"

"Because she was my wife." The words seemed to hang in the air, like the echo of a church bell. "I loved being married. I loved going out with her and saying to someone, 'Meet my wife, Maggie.' Loved it when she introduced me as her husband. Men have this bad reputation about being afraid of marriage. I wasn't. Marrying her was the best thing I ever did."

Eleanor looked at him without smiling. "Now tell me...what was the worst part of being Daniel Part One."

Once again he knew the answer in an instant.

"Maggie."

Eleanor didn't seem the least shocked. "Why?"

Daniel slowly exhaled as he adjusted the pillow behind his back. "She was thirty-nine when we got married. Turned forty on our honeymoon. And her career was so important to her."

He saw realization dawning in Eleanor's bright green eyes.

"God, Daniel... You wanted kids, didn't you?"

It seemed like a betrayal of Maggie's memory to even say it aloud. But with Eleanor, he couldn't hold anything back.

"I did. She didn't. I finally worked up the courage to suggest adoption...it didn't go over well. And the next week, she had her yearly physical and..."

"Cancer."

Daniel nodded. "Sort of a moot point then."

Eleanor inched closer to him and raised her hand to his face. With fingers both gentle and knowing, she traced his jawline, his lips, his forehead.

"You know, even if I left him, or even if he died and I was free..." she paused and seemed to steel herself. "Daniel, I never would have had your children."

His eyes flew open wide. "Elle—"

She shook her head. "I don't want to get married, and I don't want to have kids."

"I don't believe that. Not for one second."

"Why? Because that's what you want, and you can't imagine someone wanting something different? If I did want to get married and have kids, it would be with him. Not you."

"Why are you—"

"Saying this? Because it's true, and you need to know it. What you and I had was perfect. But it's easy for something to be perfect when it only has to be perfect for seven days. What you and Maggie had was a marriage. What he and I have is also a kind of marriage. But you and me? That was just a honeymoon."

Her words sank into him like the blade of a heavy knife.

"You're as much of a sadist as he is, you know." Daniel hoped she couldn't hear the agony behind the joke.

"I've picked up a few tips from Blondie on that front." She exhaled and smiled. "But I'm really not trying to hurt you. I want to help you. You have to let me go. You know I'm not what you really want. You loved being a husband. You want kids. You're not going to get that with me."

He said nothing, only stared past her. The bed shifted and out of the corner of his eye he watched her get dressed. She dragged her skirt over her hips, slipped into low heels, and buttoned up her blouse without once wincing or flinching from the welts he'd inflicted on her. Twenty-five years old and the girl was already an old pro.

"You know you'd make an incredible domina-trix," Daniel said as Eleanor came back to the bed.

She crossed her arms over her ample chest and raised one eyebrow. "You think so?"

"Definitely."

"Last time you told me I should be a writer."

Daniel shrugged. "You could always do both."

Tilting her head to the side she hummed a moment and tapped her chin.

"I've heard worse ideas. But forget about what I should do. What are you going to do?"

"Let you go...if that's what you want me to do."

"What I want is for you to be happy. You won't be happy with me." She ran a hand through his hair again and he felt the affection in her touch, the respect. But no love. Not the kind of love he wanted or needed. "So the question is...what do you want to do?"

Daniel released a mirthless laugh. "Your owner asked me the very same thing the day I buried Maggie."

"I hope you have a different answer."

He paused before answering.

"You're right," he said, finally. "I do want to get married again. I want somebody to have kids with. God, I don't even care if they're mine or hers or adopted or foster kids. I just want a houseful of children. Always have."

"You're only thirty-eight." She touched his cheek. "And rich. And you're about as sexy as it gets. There are women in this world who'd let you knock them up just to have your DNA inside them for nine months."

He sighed and shook his head. "I'm going to miss you. And when I stop missing you, I'm going to miss missing you," Daniel said and prayed that made sense to her.

"I don't love you. But I sort of wish I did. I hope that helps."

"It does a little. But just a little."

"I have to go now. Slumber party with the King."

Daniel nearly groaned aloud at the surge of envy that rushed through him. "Doesn't Kingsley have enough subs to keep him company?"

"Yeah, but they're all shit. Anya's the only good female submissive he's brought home in two years and she's off-limits."

"Anya? A good submissive? She's the most temperamental woman I've ever met," he said. He got out of bed, started to dress. "Loathed me on sight."

Eleanor looked genuinely taken aback by that. "Really? She's about the sweetest person I've ever met. Too sweet to be hanging around with deviants like us. Of course, I could say the same to you. Was she rude to you?"

"Extremely."

"Hmm...interesting. Sounds like she's got a crush."

He doubted that. Attraction and affection were two very different things. "Doesn't matter. Off-limits, like you said. Stupid auction."

"Very stupid auction. The girl is fucking terrified out of her mind about it. Even Kingsley told

her she didn't have to do it. But she's determined to
go through with it. Last virgin in one of Kingsley's
auctions walked off with two-hundred and fifty-six
thousand dollars, and that girl wasn't half as beautiful as Anya."

"I hope somebody can talk some sense into
her."

"You should try."

He gave her a stern stare. "You know I'm the
dominant in the room. Not you."

Eleanor cocked an eyebrow at him and he saw
a smile twitch at the corner of her mouth. Raising
her chin, she strode toward him and stopped only
a foot in front of him.

"Is that so?" she asked with quiet menace.
"You're the dominant here?"

He took one step forward so only inches separated them. He gave her his very best Ouch stare.

"I am."

Without any warning, Eleanor's hand shot out
and slapped him quickly across the cheek just
hard enough to sting, just light enough to be in-
sulting.

"Then act like it," she said.

She'd slapped him. Actually slapped him. He'd
slapped Maggie a thousand times just like that—
quick and wicked, hard enough to get her attention, not hard enough to actually hurt. A perfect
dominant's slap.

He needed that.

"I will."

Daniel pushed Eleanor against the wall and kissed the breath out of her. His tongue invaded her mouth and her head fell back in surrender, taking the kiss like a well-deserved punishment. Finally, he released her.

"Okay." She panted the word as he let her go. "You're the dom in the room."

"That's better."

"But you should still talk to Anya."

Daniel laughed out loud. Maybe someday he would find a woman to love him and marry him and have children with him. But he would never forget her.

"Yes, Mistress."

Eleanor finished straightening her clothes, took a deep breath, and nodded.

"I better go," she said. She left his bedroom and headed for the front door. Opening it, she paused and looked back at him. "I will miss you. I did miss you...for a long time. Longer than I'll admit to."

"I promise I'll stop loving you," Daniel said. "But it'll hurt."

"Only until you fall in love again. Then you'll thank me for leaving."

"Maybe," he said, "But not yet."

She merely gave him one last smile before walking out of his apartment and out of his life.

Forever.

The night was long and lonely, but Daniel survived it. He woke up in the bed where he and Eleanor had made love. He searched out her scent on the sheets but couldn't find it. She hadn't been there long enough to leave any trace. It was as if she'd never been there at all.

He felt okay though. Not great but okay. Was that a sign that he hadn't really been in love with her? It dawned on him that morning he might have been in love with his dream of her and losing her hurt as much as waking up from a dream.

Maybe. Maybe not. But he was wide awake now.

He got up, got dressed, had enough breakfast for two men. Then he hailed a cab and headed to Kingsley's. Why? He didn't expect Eleanor to be there. He wasn't going to see her, just to tell Kingsley it was over, for good. If only to hear himself say it out loud, to make it official. Daniel had been wrong, Kingsley right. His integrity demanded he admit it. And it wouldn't hurt to do a little commiserating, too. Nobody commiserated better than Kingsley Edge.

Daniel arrived around mid-morning and rang the bell at the front door. No answer. Very likely Kingsley was still asleep. The man was either fearless or liked to pretend he was, so Daniel wasn't surprised to find the door was unlocked. He stepped inside the entryway and looked around. Usually the place was packed but then again, usually Daniel visited in the afternoon or evening. The house was eerily empty, eerily quiet and he wondered if this is what it was like every morning when the deviants of Manhattan were still sleeping it off.

In the quiet, he heard the soft rumble of a man's voice coming from the music room. Daniel would have ignored it—probably just one of Kingsley's friends taking a call in there—except he heard another voice replying. A woman's voice. He would have minded his own business except he recognized her soft accent—it was Anya.

Daniel went to the music room and stopped at the threshold. He stood just outside the door and eavesdropped.

"Has Edge set a reserve?" a male voice inquired. Daniel didn't need to see the man to know he was older—fifties or sixties. He could tell from the timbre of his voice, the supreme self-confidence possessed only by wealthy middle-aged white men. God, Daniel hoped he never sounded like that.

"No, sir," Anya replied. She sounded meek which surprised him. He hadn't thought she had a meek bone in her body. "I think I heard the bell. I need to—"

"They can wait. If you'd rather not bother with the auction, we can settle things now," the man continued. "We'd have to have an exam, of course."

"An exam?" Her voice shook and Daniel realized she wasn't being meek at all. Rather, she was scared.

"I wouldn't buy a car without having someone check under the hood first, of course." The man chuckled. Daniel had heard enough. He pushed the door open and Anya turned and looked at him, first in surprise and then with obvious relief. She stood with her back to the fireplace, all the way back against it as if she'd been pushed there. The man—yes, white, middle-aged, bloated and pompous, wearing an expensive suit—had trapped her there. As Daniel burst into the room, the man dropped his hand from Anya's reddened face. She looked like she was about to start crying.

"Anya? You all right?" Daniel asked.

"Excuse me, but who are you?" the man demanded. He stood up straight, arms behind his back like some sort of parody of a military commander.

"I'm Daniel. Anya's helping me with a suit. We had an appointment."

"Yes," she said quickly, "we did. I'm sorry, I forgot. Mr. Harpring stopped by and I...I lost track of time."

"It's fine," Daniel said. "I'm early. Should we go?" He held out his arm and waved as if beckoning a scared child or animal to his side. Without hesitation, she walked to him, almost running. She didn't take his hand or his arm but she did something better—she stood behind his shoulder, as if trusting him to protect her. Like a shield.

"I'm happy to let Anya go with you but we hadn't quite finished our conversation yet," the man, Mr. Harpring said. "Could you give us a few minutes? Please?" He said "please" as if it were a joke, as if men like him didn't say "please" unless they were in a mood to be funny.

"I believe Anya was finished with the conversation. Weren't you?" He glanced over his shoulder. She nodded. Her face was still bright red. "She says you're done. Ready?"

He addressed the question to Anya.

"Ready," she said. "My tape measure is upstairs."

"Anya, I think your friend can wait," Mr. Harpring said. "Can't you...who are you anyway?"

Daniel wished now he was wearing a suit, not jeans and a t-shirt. In a suit, he would have put this pompous prick to shame.

"No one you want to know," Daniel said. "But don't I know you? Ron Harpring? Of Harpring, Harrison, and Jones? The law firm in Midtown?"

The man said nothing.

"My wife was an attorney," Daniel said. "Maggie Caldwell. You know that name?"

Mr. Harpring didn't answer but his eyes had widened slightly in recognition. Corporate law in Manhattan was a very small fishbowl full of sharks.

"Being married to an attorney," Daniel said, "I know as many lawyers as I do actual people. Do I need to remind you that you could be disbarred for solicitation, which—last time I checked—was illegal in this state?"

"There's no crime in bidding on a prize in a charity auction for a good cause."

Daniel doubted the man even knew what "good cause" the money was going to. "Didn't I hear you say you wanted Anya to undergo a medical exam to make sure she's virginal enough for you?"

Mr. Harpring raised his hands in surrender—mock surrender. "A man is allowed to flirt with a pretty girl. And joke around, like I did. But since you're busy, Miss Anya, I'll go. See you the night of the auction. Wear pink, if you don't mind. I love pink."

He winked and left the music room. Obviously this wasn't his first time at Kingsley's—he left by the alley door, the private door.

When he was gone, Anya exhaled heavily and sat down hard onto the sofa's black leather ottoman.

"Now you see why I was trying to talk you out of this? You really want a sleaze like that to be your first time? Did you finally come to your senses or are you still planning on going through with this idiotic auction?"

She looked up at him with wide eyes. Wide and wounded. Immediately he hated himself for going on the attack with her. She wore a white sundress and a white lace headband that made her look like a half-grown child, ready for a picnic in the park.

"I'm sorry," he said. "I'm sorry. I just...I hate men like that."

She blinked away tears. "So do I." Her voice shook. Daniel realized he was looming over her. He went down on his knees in front of her. He put his hand by her leg—by it, but not touching it. Just a hand that she could take if she wanted.

"Hey, he's gone now."

"Now," she said and shrugged. "He wanted to see if there was a reserve price on me. Or if I'd be interested in a..." She made a disgusted face. "A pre-sale."

"He wanted to scare you," Daniel said softly, very softly. "I know the type. He gets off on it."

She looked at the floor.

"I'll talk to King. I'll make sure he's not at the auction," Daniel said.

She met his eyes. "I can tell him. I don't need you to do it for me."

Exhaling, he stood up. "All right. I get it. You

don't want my help. You're an adult. I'll leave you alone."

Though he hated walking away from her, sitting there still shaking, he did. He started for the door, not as a bluff but because she was right. She could tell Kingsley herself what had happened. She didn't need him—clearly didn't want him, either. She was an adult.

He reached the door but stopped when she spoke two words in a small voice.

"Thank you."

What was this? A crack in the ice? A thaw? Or just politeness?

"You're welcome," he said, then started to leave again.

"I do need to measure you again," she said. "For your suit. The jacket is pieced together at Signore's."

"I'll call and make an appointment." He wanted to say more, do more. He didn't want to push, however, and have her push him away again. But he couldn't stop himself from asking, "Do you need a cab? Ride home? I can have King's driver take you to work if you're going in today."

"I'm on front door duty here," she said. "This is my other job."

"How many jobs do you have?"

"Not enough." She gave him a slight smile.

"I suppose if I offered to give you some money you'd hate me, right? Hypothetically?"

She nodded, though the smile remained on her lips.

"Stubborn women. What is it with me and stubborn women?" he said.

"What is it with you and stubborn women?" Anya asked.

"I like them. Against my better judgment."

That got a little laugh out of her. "I'm not stubborn. There's a difference between stubborn and, you know...determined."

"And that is?"

"I don't know but there has to be a difference, yes? Why would they be two different words if there wasn't?"

"Good point." He turned again, looked at the door, knew he should go out it.

He didn't.

"It's only this...I know a lot of kinky guys," Daniel said. "And some are great and some aren't. You don't get to pick your winning bidder."

"I know."

"And I'm no sub but I know it's a lot of work, a lot of trust putting yourself into someone else's hands and if you don't know that person and you've never done it before—"

"I've done it before."

Daniel looked at her, shocked. "You've done it before? Kink? I thought—"

"I didn't have sex with him. I just did, you know... I submitted to him."

A smile of pride played across her sweet pink

lips. She blushed lightly. His body temperature went up a degree or two. Or ten.

"Monsieur," she whispered. "Just once."

Kingsley. That lucky French bastard.

"What did he do to you?"

She shook her head. "Nothing. He didn't even touch me."

"He doesn't have to touch you to dominate you. Anya," Daniel said again, this time in his sternest voice. "What did he do to you? Tell me."

Her face turned scarlet at what must have been a potent memory. Daniel's pulse raced and his groin tightened at the thoughts running through his head, the various scenarios. He could easily think of ten or twelve things he'd love to make Anya submit to–acts that would leave her a virgin but certainly a great deal less innocent.

"He...watched me."

Daniel's head swam at the image those three words conjured. The first time he saw Anya in her little sailor dress...those high heels with her lacy bobby socks... He could just see her reaching under her dress and pulling her panties down and off. Knowing Kingsley, he would have made her give them to him. Kingsley would have ordered her to lay down on the bed or on one of his fainting couches. He would have stood over her and watched as she pulled her dress up to her hips, opened her legs, and began touching herself.

"Kingsley ordered you to masturbate for him. And you did it?"

"*Oui.*" Her voice was hardly more than a whisper. But he heard it.

"You enjoyed submitting to him, to that?"

"It was...it was everything I wanted it to be. Except, you know, maybe not with him. But I know I'll be fine when the time comes."

"You think you'll be fine letting a total stranger order you around, beat you, and fuck you? He could be a sadist, a blood-play fetishist. He could be into rape-play or breath-play. Or worse he could be as ugly and Canadian as I am."

Anya laughed nervously. "I'll survive one night."

"Do you really want to be in this auction? Really?"

She was silent a moment, then said, "No. But I need to be in it."

"You don't need—How about a loan? You can pay me back whenever—ten years, twenty years—"

"Daniel, no." She shook her head. Slowly she stood up from the ottoman and stood by the cold empty fireplace. "I know you think you're trying to help me."

"I am. I just want to help you. Nothing else."

"It is...very *nice* of you."

Daniel nearly laughed at how long she paused before forcing the word "nice" out.

"But?"

"But I've made up my mind. One night with one man and me and my brothers and sisters will all be free. I'll be able to go home and buy a little house and they can all come live with me. What- ever it takes, I'll do it, and I won't regret it."

Free, she said. He understood though he wished he didn't. She wanted to be free. If she took the money from him, she'd be beholden to him.

"It's not the same, just being watched while you make yourself come and actually really doing kink with somebody. It's night and day. It'll be someone else touching you and you might not like how they—"

"Stop. Please."

The "please" was soft. He was scaring her. She ought to be scared, he thought. But still...he didn't want to scare her. So he stopped.

"I'll only say one more thing—whatever price anyone pays for it, for you, it wouldn't be enough."

"Ah, true," she said with a smile. "But it would be better than nothing."

He'd tried. There was nothing else to do.

"I'll see you later," he said.

"You will?"

"At Vitale's?"

She smiled nervously. "Right. Yes. See you then."

For the third time, he turned to leave. The door was right there, just a few steps away. He'd almost made it when Anya spoke again, stopping him dead in his tracks.

"Maybe you can help me?"

He looked at her, her back still to the white fireplace mantel. Her face was pink again.

"You said it's different, really doing kink with someone? Maybe, you know...we could practice?"

Daniel blinked once.

"Yes," he said. "I could help you with that."

He locked the door.

———

ANYA'S EYES WIDENED. Her amber eyes. Daniel knew all about amber, fossilized tree resin. A famous geologist had left his life's work to the New York Public Library and it had been Daniel's job to catalog every page, every piece, including a large chunk of bright clear amber that held inside it a million-year-old butterfly. He'd wanted to free it. Like now. Like he wanted to free Anya, to melt the amber she was trapped inside and watch the beautiful little prisoner spread her wings and fly.

First he would need heat.

Daniel walked over to Anya who backed up so far against the fireplace she almost stepped into the grate. Only an inch separated their bodies.

"Now?" Anya asked, breathless.

"Now. See? You agree to submit to me, and you give up your power. I say when, not you. You like it? You can tell me no."

"So far it's not so bad." Her voice shook.

Not so bad? It was a start.

Daniel felt the enormous weight of responsibility settle onto his shoulders. But—according to Anya—he had broad shoulders. He hoped they were broad enough to carry her over this threshold and not let her fall.

"You have a safe word?"

"It's um…Leonard."

He almost laughed. "Leonard?"

"It's my cat's name. I found him in an alley on an old blue coat someone had thrown away."

"Ah. Leonard Cohen." He knew the song well, "Famous Blue Raincoat." Leonard Cohen was one of Canada's most famous exports. Leonard Cohen. Maple syrup. Hockey.

"My mother sang his songs all the time. To us. To herself. To nobody. Now I sing his songs to Leonard. I don't know why I'm telling you all this."

She was nervous, talking to cover it. He wanted her to keep talking, to tell him all her secrets. He wanted to know everything there was to know about this lovely lonely girl who sang "Famous Blue Raincoat" to the alley cat she'd rescued.

"You're allowed to talk," he said. "Until I say you can't. How does that make you feel?"

He moved closer so that their bodies touched. Her cheek brushed his shoulder. His hips brushed her stomach.

"Scared?"

"Good. Fear can your save your life."

"I feel safe, too. I don't know how that can work. Doesn't make sense, but it's true." She met his eyes, briefly, then looked down to the floor.

"Because you are safe." He put his mouth to her ear and whispered, "For now."

A shiver passed through her. Daniel saw it, felt it, relished it. He raised his hand to her face and brushed her cheek. It was burning hot.

"What do you fantasize about when you make yourself come?"

Anya laughed—loud and sudden. A shocked laugh that she tried to cover with a nervous giggle.

"What?"

"You heard me." No mercy. No quarter. If she wanted to go through with this stupid auction, he would make certain she knew what she was getting herself into.

"I can't—"

"Yes, you can. This is submission, Anya. I'm in charge. You put me in charge. I ask the questions. You answer them. I give the orders. You take them. I spank and you are spanked. I flog and you are flogged. I whip and you are whipped. I bite and you are bitten. I kiss and you open your mouth and let me kiss you until you've forgotten how to do anything but everything I want you to do."

He put his lips to her cheek at her ear, then kissed, but only there, on her cheek.

"Are you going to kiss me?" she asked. "Really kiss me?"

"Haven't decided yet."

"I want you to."

"I don't care."

She exhaled loudly.

He could barely stop himself from laughing. "Why should I kiss you? You haven't earned it yet."

She leaned a little closer to him. Any closer and she'd be standing on his toes. "How do I earn it?"

"Call me 'sir' for starters." He placed his hands on her hips, around her narrow waist. The muscles of her stomach tightened when he touched her. He could feel her every breath.

"Sir," she said. "There?"

"Better. Not good enough, but an improvement."

She made that sound of purest frustration again. Delicious.

"Are we having fun yet?" he taunted.

"You make me so mad."

"Then I'm doing it right. And you forgot to call me 'sir.' And you still haven't answered my question. You have five seconds to do both, or I'll do something cruel and terrible to you."

"What?"

"I'll leave without kissing you. Four... three...two—"

"You, sir."

He pulled back and looked down at her face. She met his eyes very briefly before lowering them.

"You think about me when you come?" He couldn't have come up with a better answer himself.

"Last night. Sir."

"What was I doing to you?"

Her pink cheeks turned crimson. "You were, ah...flogging me and I was tied up and then we, you know."

"Made love?"

She was shivering in his arms. He held her closer, tighter. He was hard and hungry for her but knew he had to hold back.

"Yes," she finally said. "*Sir*."

"Good. Now you've earned your kiss."

She raised her face to his and he pressed his mouth to hers. The kiss was soft at first, as he explored her top lip, then the bottom. He could feel her heart beating against his chest. Poor little girl. She had no idea how much he could make her feel if she would only let him.

He forced her mouth wider and slipped his tongue inside her. She moaned and he made it worse by sliding his hand down her back and then up again, under the skirt of her sundress. He cupped her bottom, slipping his fingers under her panties to stroke one soft, warm cheek. He wanted to hold her pussy in his hands, cradle it, stroke it until she was begging for him to be inside her. Whether she realized it or not, she was pushing her hips into his. If that's what she wanted, he would give it to her.

Daniel wrapped his arms around her and lifted her off the floor, settling her against his hips and pinning her back to the mantel. She gasped against his mouth but didn't break the kiss. He pushed his hips into hers and she pushed back. If they'd been naked, they'd be fucking. Instead they worked against each other through their clothes. His cock was hard and her panties were flimsy. He knew she could feel his erection. He could feel the heat of her pussy against him. He worked his hips harder into her soft mound as he deepened the kiss. Deeper. Harder. Faster. He wanted to overwhelm her with sensation, need.

He carried her to the sofa, pushed her onto her back and laid on top of her, only breaking the kiss long enough to make her want it again. He found her mouth, her tongue...he rubbed his erection against her softness. She opened her legs wider. Her fingers gripped the back of his shirt and dug in. So close...almost there. Her breathing was hard and heavy.

Someone knocked on the door.

Anya gasped and looked at the door. Daniel sat up. Before he could say a word, she scrambled out from under him and ran to the door.

She opened it and there stood Kingsley in the doorway, looking rakishly disheveled, like a pirate who'd spent the night with a duke and stolen his clothes the next morning. Shirt unbuttoned to the collarbone, hair down, bare feet.

"Hello," he said. "Am I interrupting?"

"No," Anya said quickly. Too quickly.

"Are we sure?" Kingsley looked straight at Daniel.

"Some asshole named Harpring came by,"

Daniel explained. "He was harassing Anya. I locked him out." He was doing his best to sit casually on the couch and not look like a man who'd been seconds away from coming one minute ago. He doubted Kingsley was fooled.

"Harassing you?" Kingsley scowled. "Did he hurt you?"

"No, he was only being disgusting. Daniel sent him away."

"Good," Kingsley said. "Never liked him anyway."

"I don't want him at the auction, if you don't mind, *monsieur*," she said.

"*C'est la vie*," Kingsley said. "Whatever you say. There will be plenty of others." He gave Daniel a look that was almost a wink.

"He might come back."

"Anya, you can go up to my office and work on the files instead. If anyone comes to the door, we'll just ignore them today."

Anya nodded and started to leave. When she stepped into the hallway, she glanced back—not at Kingsley, but at him. Daniel smiled. She smiled in return then went quickly up the stairs. Daniel watched her until she disappeared through the door on the second floor. It was physically painful to pretend indifference, to stay there and not follow her, to kiss her again. But he didn't want her getting in trouble with Kingsley.

"Well," Kingsley said. "That didn't take long."

Daniel glared at him. "We were talking."

"Her lips were swollen. Were you talking for ten hours?"

"I was trying to talk her out of being in your stupid auction."

"Talk her out of it or fuck her out of it?"

Daniel smiled. "Five more minutes and I would have done it."

"Five more seconds, I think."

"Guess I'll never know, thanks to you. Great timing."

"Have you ever thought that perhaps...you should let her do what she wants? Women like that, I hear."

"First of all, I don't think she wants to do it. I think she thinks she needs to do it. And second, I'm not going to take relationship advice from a man who calls his girlfriends his 'collection.' Makes you sound like a fucking serial killer with a cellar full of bodies."

"It's a joke. And they're not girlfriends. They're simply friends I have enormous amounts of sex with." He shrugged. "Enough about me. Our mutual friend told me Elle paid you a visit."

"She did." Daniel stood up. His erection was long gone by now, thanks to Kingsley. If it wasn't, mention of Elle would have dealt the death blow.

"And?"

"She dumped me. Again."

"Not surprised but, for what it's worth, you have my sympathy. She is very special. You know, the way volcanoes are very special."

"Volcanoes?"

"They're beautiful, you don't run across them often, and you're always happy to get away from one with your life."

Daniel laughed. He hadn't thought he could laugh over losing Elle but he already was, one day later.

"Well, I'm alive," Daniel said. "It's over. You can tell our 'mutual friend' I won't try stealing his girl-friend ever again."

"He'll be glad to hear that. I'm certain he was shaking in his shoes."

"It's not my fault she has bad taste in men."

Kingsley laughed softly. "I'll tell him you said that, too. He'll be very hurt. He might even cry."

Daniel met him at the door. "Has anyone ever told you that sarcasm isn't sexy?"

"When you're sexy, everything you say is sexy."

"Say 'Massachusetts,'" Daniel said. "I dare you."

Maggie had told Daniel long ago that Kings-ley's English was perfect, except for his one Achilles heel—Massachusetts.

"Can't do it, can you?"

"I live in New York for a reason." Then he cleared his throat. "Mass-a-shoo—"

"I knew it."

"Now I know why Anya hates you so much."

"One of many reasons. You'll keep on eye her, right?"

"You care about her, don't you?"

"I couldn't save Maggie. Eleanor didn't want saved. Do I get to help one beautiful girl in my life? Just one? Too much to ask?"

Kingsley glanced up and Daniel followed his gaze. Anya was peeking over the staircase bannister down at them, eavesdropping. He didn't mind. He'd been eavesdropping on her earlier. When they caught her looking, she straightened up.

"I have a question about the files," she said to Kingsley.

A smile spread across Kingsley's face. "I'll be right up." She disappeared. Kingsley met Daniel's eyes. "Do you trust me?"

"Not as far as I could throw ten of you to Massachusetts."

"Ah, fair. But I'm going to help you anyway."

Kingsley patted his shoulder and sauntered toward the stairs. As he walked away, Daniel issued a plea.

"Please don't."

8

Two days passed. Long days. Daniel had meetings to keep him occupied—lawyer, accountant, financial advisor. Being rich was a full-time job, Maggie had warned him. True. Not that he was nostalgic at all for his salad days. Between being rich and being broke, well, it wasn't a competition at all. Look at Anya, working two jobs and selling herself to a stranger in one week's time to get her brothers and sisters out from under the thumb of an angry alcoholic father. Anyone who romanticized poverty had never been poor. But...he did sometimes miss having a real job. When he jogged past the Stephen A. Schwarzman building where he used to work, he was hit by a wave of nostalgia. The library was just opening for the day. Not too many tourists there yet in the Rose Reading Room to be offended by his sweaty t-shirt and track pants.

Daniel jogged up the stairs and once inside the scent of wood polish and old books hit him like a truck. He almost had to sit down, the memories washed over him so hard, so fast. The day he got the job at the most famous branch of any library in all of the United States of America...calling his parents from a payphone to let them know he was going to be okay, that they didn't have to worry about him anymore...first day at work, taking the tour with Suzette Mayer who'd worked there for fifty years, knew every nook, every book, everything there was to know about the place and tried to teach it all to him in one day...

Boxes of dust. That's what she gave him for his first task. So it seemed at least when he pulled off the parcel tape and a cloud of dust wafted into his face. He sneezed for five straight minutes before he went back to the box and found the papers of a famous dead poet inside, papers that had been moldering in a New England attic for eighty years. Suzette said they'd been saving that box for the "new kid." Lucky him.

He was lucky. He loved the work, the quiet hours, the digging deep into the past like an archeologist-slash-treasure hunter. He did find treasure. Loads of it. The missing last will and testament of a long-dead industrialist, one that changed the life of a distant descendant. A first draft of an Emily Dickinson poem jotted on the back of an envelope. A previously unknown love letter from Georgia O'Keeffe to Arthur Stieglitz.

Daniel had brought Maggie here on one of their early dates, at night, using his key to let them into a staff door around the back. The place was empty but for the security guard and the cleaning crew. He'd taken her up to the third floor, to one of the Rare Books Rooms. He'd only brought her there to show off. The library was legendary. A work of art in itself. The Rare Books Room contained a million dollars' worth of books and he had the key to the cases. She'd been dazzled. Though a life-long New Yorker, she'd never seen the hidden rooms of the library. Sure, she worked in a Manhattan skyscraper with people who made more money in a day than he made in a year but had she ever been to the secret storage room where all the Victorian-era pornography was hidden away, brought out only for authors and grad students doing "research?"

He remembered it like yesterday. It had been the first time they'd had sex. Here, in the library. First kiss in the Rose Reading Room. Second kiss as they turned the pages of a photo album full of sepia-colored photographs from a birching club that had been in business around the turn-of-the-century. Men being spanked. Women been whipped. By the time they made it up to the Rare Books Room, Daniel was dying to have her. He'd kissed her there too, after shutting and locking the door.

The entire time he'd been fucking her he couldn't believe this incredibly beautiful obviously over-educated older woman had her legs wrapped around his twenty-five-year-old back and was tight enough around him to clench his cock like a hand. He had put his hand over Maggie's lips to silence her moans. He had pushed a finger into her mouth and told her to bite him if she needed him to stop —otherwise he wouldn't. She didn't, and neither did he, and he came inside her so hard he'd almost blacked out.

After the sex, she'd done something even more wicked than fuck a librarian in his own library. She'd taken a pencil and one of the rare books—a first edition, first printing of *Moby Dick*, worth about fifty-thousand dollars—and written inside the back cover, *Daniel Caldwell is a great lay.* When he'd told her she was on the hook for fifty grand, she said she could afford it. When he told her she could get him fired for that, she promised she'd take the blame.

Daniel wondered...was it still there? He hadn't erased it, worried he'd do the old book more harm than good. He took the stairs up the to the third floor and into the Rare Books Room. There was the big oak table where he'd had Maggie all those years ago. There was the barrister bookcase. There was the book. She'd only picked it because it had "Dick" in the title. The bookcase was locked and he'd long ago turned in his keys. He knew he should let it go, just enjoy the memory but for some reason, he wanted to see Maggie's hand-writing again.

He found one of the librarians who'd worked there during his tenure. They chatted a few minutes and by the end, it was nothing to ask her to open the bookcase for him. He explained he was thinking of buying a first edition of *Moby Dick,* that he'd seen one in an antiques store but wanted to make sure it was the real thing. She happily unlocked the case for him and left him alone with the book and a pair of cotton gloves.

Carefully he opened the book and turned to the end pages. There it was, *Daniel Caldwell is a great lay.*

That wasn't all that was there, however. Under those words was written something else, also in Maggie's handwriting.

Daniel, if you're reading this, I'm gone. Please find love again and get married again. I can rest in peace if I know you're happy, my love. You're too good a lay to waste.

The words took the breath from his body. He laughed, then cried, then laughed again, all alone up in the Rare Books Room where they'd made love so many years ago on that very table. If someone saw him now, what would they think? That he just really loved the ending of *Moby Dick*?

Maggie must have come back at some point, gotten the book off the shelf—had she told the same lie?—and written him that note before she got too sick to go out on her own. She knew him so well, knew how nostalgic he was, how sentimental. She knew he'd come back here someday and remember that wild night he'd snuck her into this beautiful room to ravish her, surrounded by the greatest works of literature in history. Or maybe she didn't know. Maybe she guessed. Maybe if he looked, he'd find this same note written all over the city, in all their old haunts.

Get married again? Too good a lay to waste? That was Maggie.

"I'll try, my love," he whispered to the secret words.

Daniel took a photo of the message with his phone camera and then put the book back. He didn't erase the words. Knowing what he knew about Herman Melville, the old rascal would have appreciated his book being used to pass a lusty love note across time and from beyond the grave.

When he left the library and returned to the city, he felt like he'd been given a gift.

Energized by that gift, by that last message from Maggie, he jogged all the way home. It would be good for him to wear himself out. Sleep had been elusive since coming back to the city. Maybe if he could exhaust himself physically, he wouldn't dream about Anya like he had last night, and the night before... As his shoes pounded the pavement, he imagined Harpring's face under the soles. He imagined every man who would bid on Anya the night of the auction being pummeled under his feet.

Still drenched with sweat from his run, Daniel decided to take a long, hot bath to help ease the soreness from his legs before going back out again.

He started running the water but had to shut it off when he heard the doorbell chime.

"Who is it?" he called out before he reached the door.

"Celine Dion."

Daniel was so shocked at the sound of her voice that his mind went momentarily blank. He recovered his senses and swung the door open. Anya was wearing a pale pink empire-waist sundress, her hair in two small buns on each side of her head like Princess Leia.

She didn't meet his eyes. "I'm being punished."

Daniel laughed. He couldn't help it. "Kingsley's punishing you?"

Anya nodded sheepishly.

"Why?"

She sighed. "I was at his house reading on the floor. On my stomach. He saw me and asked me what I was doing."

"And you said?" Daniel asked, picturing Anya lying prone on the floor and rather enjoying the image.

"I said I was doing my impression of Paris during the Nazi Occupation."

Daniel nearly died holding his laughter in. Anya had all the makings of a S.A.M.—a Smart-Ass Masochist. He didn't want to encourage such terrible—if hilarious—bad behavior.

"Kingsley should be punishing you, not me."

"He said he was too busy."

Kingsley was never too busy to punish a beautiful girl for having a smart mouth. It was one of his favorite hobbies. That meant only one thing—Kingsley was making good on his promise to "help" Daniel. How? By playing matchmaker? Apparently so.

"What's your punishment? Is he making you come cook lunch for me or something?"

"He said I had to do whatever you told me to do for the next two hours. Except—"

"I can't have sex with you. Obviously." Daniel considered his options. Anya wanted him—fact. But she didn't want him enough to let him help her—also a fact. Maybe he could change that.

"Look, you don't have to stay. I'll tell Kingsley I made you mop the floors on your hands and knees. He'll never know."

Her eyes widened. "You want me to go?"

"No, but I imagine you wouldn't mind two hours off."

He was baiting her, making her choose him. Cruel? A little but a little cruelty was just his style when it came to beautiful submissive women who drove him up the wall.

"It wouldn't be right if I didn't get punished. I have been very bad." It looked to Daniel like she was having trouble saying that with a straight face.

"Then I suppose I should punish you. Since you know you deserve it. Come in."

She eased across the threshold and stood in the middle of his living room, looking around without speaking. She looked nervous. Good. He was about to make her even more nervous.

"It's nice to see you again," he said. "I'm sorry we were interrupted two days ago."

Her hands were clasped behind her back. She shrugged as if the whole thing were forgotten.

"Did you come last night while fantasizing about me?" he asked.

Her cheeks reddened. Had any woman ever blushed more beautifully?

"I only said that to make you kiss me," she said. "When you're kissing me you don't talk so much."

"Ah, I see." He nodded. "Makes sense. I was thinking of you when I came last night. In case you were wondering."

She stared at her shoes. "You did?"

"I did. Do you want me to tell you what I was fantasizing about?"

She lifted her eyes to his but quickly lowered them again. "It wouldn't be a good idea."

This made him unreasonably happy. Maybe she wanted him enough that he could convince her to let him help her.

Help her.

Fuck her.

All of the above.

"Then I suppose I better start punishing you," he said. "Come with me."

"Where are we going?"

"Bathroom."

"What are we doing in your bathroom?"

"I'm taking a bath. And you are going to help."

———

ANYA FOLLOWED Daniel to his bathroom and didn't say a single word the entire walk there. Not a word of complaint. Not a word of insult. Either she was scared or she was excited.

In the bathroom, he shut the door. "Scared?" he asked, turning the tap back on.

She lifted her chin. "Of course not."

"Really?"

She clasped her hands nervously in front of her and rubbed an invisible speck of something off her thumb.

"I have three brothers. I changed their diapers and helped them dress for school. You don't have anything that will surprise me, Daniel."

Daniel grinned at her in a way he hoped made her even more nervous than she already was.

She glared at him. "Sir."

"You're submitting to me for the next two hours," he reminded her. "When you submit to me, you call me, 'sir.' *Comprenez, ma petite?*"

"Your accent is terrible."

"You forgot to call me 'sir.'"

She was silent a moment. "I don't want to do that again."

"Why not?" he asked softly. "Didn't like it?"

She didn't say anything at first. Then, finally, "I think I liked it too much."

"Too much?"

"It's not good for me to like it so much."

No, he supposed it wasn't. It wasn't good for him to like her so much, either. Off-limits, he reminded himself. Well, this was going to be awkward.

"All right," he said, shutting the water off now that the tub had filled. "Call me Daniel then."

"Daniel," she repeated. Somehow she managed to sound deferential just saying his name.

"Good. Now undress me."

Anya's eyes went wide—comically wide—but she didn't object. Instead, she crossed the floor so slowly, so gingerly, one would have thought she'd been walking barefoot across broken glass. It took everything he had not to laugh out loud at her nervousness.

Slowly Anya reached out and laid her hands flat on his stomach. Curling her fingers, she grasped the fabric of his sweat-stained t-shirt.

"You have beautiful hands," Daniel said, noticing for the first time her delicate fingers, so graceful and well-formed.

She shook her head. "I don't. See?" She released his shirt and turned her hands over letting him see her palms. All over her fingertips he saw small calluses and pinpricks from her sewing needles.

Daniel took her gently by the wrists and raised her hands to chest height. "Still beautiful...but you work too hard."

He lifted one hand to his lips and kissed the center of her palm. Anya breathed in sharply as his mouth met her skin. Under his thumb he could feel the rapid beating of her pulse.

"Now...continue." He reluctantly released her wrists, and she once again grasped the fabric of his t-shirt.

"You're disgusting, Daniel." She started to pull the shirt upward. "What were you doing?"

"Running."

"*Fou.* Madness."

"Exercise."

"Was someone chasing you?"

"Not that I saw."

"Then yes, madness. Lift your arms, *s'il vous plaît.*"

Daniel didn't move a muscle.

Anya sighed with obvious irritation. "Lift your arms...please."

He raised his arms and let Anya pull his shirt completely off. As she took it off she turned around and held the sweaty garment out in front of her.

"What are you doing, Anya?"

"Looking for an open flame so I can burn this."

Daniel laughed. "We'll have a bonfire later," he said, tossing the shirt into the corner of the steam-filled bathroom.

He stood before her shirtless. She stared at the floor. Poor girl. He really was torturing her. He'd feel bad about it if he didn't feel so good about it.

He took her wrists in his hands again and pressed her shaking palms into the center of his chest.

For nearly a full minute Daniel said nothing, simply letting Anya's anxiety build. He wanted her anxious, afraid. For her own good.

"Your hands are shaking. You're white as a ghost. Think about how you feel right now. Imagine, Anya," Daniel said in a low voice. Anya closed her eyes. "Imagine being with someone you've never even met before and doing this. Or worse. Any man who wins you will own you for the night. He might already have you tied to the bed at this point. He might already be inside you. Feel how afraid you are right now and multiply that by a thousand. At least a thousand."

Anya finally looked at him, really looked at him. First at his eyes and then his lips. From his lips her eyes roamed down his neck and across his shoulders and chest, up each arm and down his stomach before grazing up his body again to look once more into his eyes.

"I'm not afraid," she whispered. "That's not why I'm shaking."

"Not afraid? Really? Then why are you shaking?" he demanded. He had to get through to this girl before she made the worst mistake of her life.

"Because..." She stopped and swallowed again and stared at something over his shoulder.

Daniel lifted a hand to her face and caressed

her neck under her ear. "Answer the question, Anya. Why are you shaking?"

She met his gaze. "Because...I want you."

Daniel didn't speak at first. He let her confession hang in the air between them.

"Say it again," Daniel ordered.

"I want you. I can't...since that day in the music room, I can't stop thinking about you. I hate you so I must be crazy, too."

"I don't think you do hate me. I don't think you hate me at all. I think you like me." Daniel continued stroking her face, her neck just under her hairline and was rewarded with a shiver.

"I can't afford to...*like* you."

He gently grasped her chin and forced her face up to his. "Fine," he said. "Don't like me then. I'll like you enough for the both of us."

He brought his mouth down onto hers and waited. He didn't have to wait long. Anya parted her lips and let her body relax into his. Tenuously at first she kissed him. And while everything in him wanted to push her against the wall, force her lips wider, and take full possession of her mouth, he held back and let her do most of the work. He cupped the back of her head and allowed himself the liberty of pushing the tip of his tongue against hers again and again.

Finally he wrenched his mouth from hers. He'd take her right on the bathroom floor if he didn't get himself under control again. She watched him, her amber eyes wide as a frightened deer.

"No more stalling," he said. "The water will get cold."

He was dominating her right now, supposedly. He refused to let her see how much that kiss had affected him. He shouldn't be doing this with her, not with his self-control so low and his need so strong. That note he'd found from Maggie had cut him open, bared his insides, left him too vulnerable to the scared kisses of beautiful young women.

Anya's hands still shook as she knelt down on the floor in front of him. Now Daniel had to glance away. If he looked at her on her knees in front of him all hope for continued self-control would be lost. She fumbled with the laces of his running shoes. He raised one foot, then the other as she pulled them off, along with his socks. She must really be scared as she offered no commentary about burning his sweaty footwear.

As the seconds passed, Anya seemed to fall into her submissive role. She set his shoes aside neatly and tucked the laces into them. She put his socks in the far corner with his sweaty t-shirt. Daniel lost the battle of wills with himself and started watching her again. A veil seemed to fall over her eyes as the angry, scared, temperamental Anya disappeared and a new placid, contented, submissive Anya took her place. At that moment, Daniel wasn't sure which Anya he preferred.

Submissive Anya reached up and started to pull his track pants down.

That Anya. Definitely.

She kept her eyes respectfully lowered as she brought his pants all the way down. Daniel studied her as he stepped out them.

"You're beautiful to see. Just like this."

She whispered something in French and Daniel cursed himself for spending the last year and a half perfecting his Spanish and Portuguese. He even knew how to ask, "Which is the safest bush for pissing on?" in Quechua. Instead he should have been learning some damn French.

"What was that?" he asked and decided to start brushing up on his French first chance he got— that day, preferably.

"*Vous aussi*," she repeated. Anya looked up at him from the floor. Any remaining fear had disappeared from her gaze. Only innocent trust remained in her wide eyes. "You also."

Daniel said nothing, only smiled. He stepped away from her and sank into the steaming bathwater. Without even waiting for his order, Anya stood up, took off her shoes and came to the bathtub. He leaned forward to make room for her to sit on the edge of the tub behind him, then leaned back, forcing Anya to spread her legs so he could settle between her knees. When she reached for the bath sponge, he turned his head and bit her lightly on the inside of her thigh. She flinched and kicked water.

"So much for submission." Daniel grabbed a towel and wiped water off his face. "Was nice while it lasted."

"You could have warned me you were going to bite me."

"It's not as much fun if you know it's coming."

Anya huffed peevishly.

"I'm sorry," he said. "I'm trying my best. I'm...nervous."

"And I'm not making it easier on you, am I?"

"You are not. You're very attractive and very... big. Tall."

"I'm five-eleven. One inch shorter than Kingsley, remember?" he teased. "Although we're fairly well-matched in one other area."

"Is that so?" she asked. *Iz zat so?* Could her accent be any sexier? Daniel thought about it, decided the answer was no. "You've seen him naked?"

"This is Kingsley Edge we're talking about. There are only three people in the city who haven't seen him naked. And they've all been in comas since the late eighties."

Anya laughed as she started scrubbing his shoulders with the sponge. He leaned forward again to give her access to his back.

"*Monsieur* is so strange to me. His French is *parfait*. It's obvious he is from France. But his name isn't French."

"His real last name is French and it's as long as his...it's a big name. Boissonneault. And the

'Kingsley' is American because his American mother named him."

"His mother is American? I can't wait to mock him for that."

"Don't you dare."

"Why not?"

He looked up at her. "I'll get jealous. I'm the only one I want you being mean to."

Anya smiled down at him. Then she wrung the sponge out on his face.

Daniel tore the sponge from her hands and rubbed it on her face. Squealing, she raised her arms to block his assault as she let loose a stream of words that he felt reasonably certain constituted some of the worst insults in the French language. Finally he relented and threw the sponge on the floor all the way across the spacious bathroom.

"You're dangerous with that thing," he said.

"How am I supposed—"

"Use your hands."

Anya mumbled something under her breath as she picked up a bar of soap and lathered it up between her hands. Slapping her hands hard onto his wet shoulders, she began to knead his taut muscles.

"You might get better access if you joined me in the bath," Daniel said and wished he could see her face.

"I would get wet."

"That would be the plan."

Anya groaned and stood up. She walked

around him through the water and came to sit on the ledge at his side.

Daniel raised a leg out of the water and put his foot in her lap. "No tickling," he ordered.

"This dress wasn't meant to get wet, you know."

"You could take it off."

She glared at him.

"Just a suggestion. Not an order." Daniel winked at her. "You know, for someone who claims poverty and supposedly sends all her money to her brother...you dress very chic."

"I make all my clothes. This dress—"

"*Zat* dress?"

Anya stuck her tongue out at him. "*Oui, zis drezz* only took a day to make and maybe...ten dollars? Fifteen? *Maman* and I made all the little ones' clothes."

Daniel studied her dress for the first time, rather than the woman in it. Though it was a simple pink sundress, nothing about it looked cheap to his eyes.

"Have you thought about going to design school?" he asked. "Or starting your own line? You're incredibly talented."

She bent over and gathered water in her cupped hands. Pouring it over his calf and foot she merely shrugged. "Once all the children are through school, then I will think about it."

"How old is the youngest?"

"Seven."

"Seven? You're going to wait eleven years before going to school?"

Making no reply, Anya lathered up her hands again and ran her soapy fingers up and down his legs. He noted that she stopped at his knee, seemingly fearing to move farther up his leg. Probably a wise decision. Her delicate fingers on his skin both moved him to arousal and also simply...moved him. This girl was so much younger than him, so inexperienced. Had he ever been with a virgin before? No. Never. Even the girl he'd lost his virginity to had been with one person before him.

"Anya?"

"I'll be thirty-five," she said, smiling. "And I think that's a perfect age."

"I'm thirty-eight."

She released a sigh of pure disgust. "Terrible. I'll have to make you a cane."

At the word "cane," Daniel reached out and grabbed Anya by the wrist. With one tug he had her in the water. She yelped at the sudden move, but didn't fight when he forced her to straddle his thighs.

"Never say 'cane' around a dominant." Daniel wrapped his arms around her lower back and whispered into her ear, "I'll get ideas."

He held her on him, letting her feel through the lace of her panties how much he wanted her. She tried to wrench free of his tight grasp, to no avail. Until she said her safe word, he wouldn't back off an inch.

"Do you fantasize about that?" Daniel asked as he ran his hands possessively up her back, feeling the fabric of her dress dampen with his touch. "About bending over my bed while I cane you?"

She closed her eyes tight and rested her forehead on his shoulder. She didn't answer in words but he felt her nod.

Daniel slipped his other hand under her dress and let it rest high on her thigh. Her soft skin felt so smooth and warm in the steaming bath water. What he wouldn't give to have her naked against him.

Anya let out a low groan.

Daniel squeezed her thigh and let his hand inch a little higher.

Slowly, Anya wound her arms around his shoulders. He felt her hands, balled into nervous fists, finally start to unclench.

"I have a cane. Several. Want to see them?" Daniel moved his hand from her thigh to between her legs. He pressed two fingers gently against the lace of her panties. Even through the fabric he could feel her swollen clitoris. Anya stiffened but made no protest.

"Do you?" he asked again. Daniel brought his mouth to the hollow of her throat. His fingers made tight circles against her clitoris as his other hand gripped the back of her neck.

She nodded again, as if she'd lost her ability to speak. Her chest rose and fell with her rapid breaths; her small, taut nipples showed against the wet front of her dress. Over and over she thrust her hips against Daniel's fingers.

Daniel remembered the first time he fantasized about Anya in Signore Vitale's shop. He imagined fucking her from behind against the mirror. He'd vowed to himself...

"Say something nice about me," Daniel ordered. "You don't get to come until you say something nice. Now."

"I lied." The words came out immediately, hungrily.

"Lied? About what?"

"*Monsieur*...he didn't punish me by sending me to you." She closed her eyes tight and bit her bottom lip. "I just wanted to be with you again."

9

Anya's confession sent the last of Daniel's self-restraint packing. Wrapping both arms around her, he lifted her out of the bathtub. Water poured off them both as he carried her to his bedroom.

Without a trace of gentleness, he put her on her back and yanked her panties down her legs. He tugged her dress up and heard it tear as it came off her and ended up in a wet pile on the floor.

Anya arched underneath him as he took a pale pink nipple into his mouth and sucked on it while his fingers found her other nipple and kneaded it. Daniel felt Anya's hands sliding up his shoulders. He pulled back, grabbed her arms, and pinned her to the bed by her wrists. Using his knees, Daniel wrenched her thighs wide open. Only when Anya stiffened in obvious fear did he stop. Closing his eyes he took a deep slow breath to calm himself.

"Tell me this is what you want," he said in a low voice. "Say it."

"I want you, sir." Her voice sounded so small, so scared. "I want you inside me."

He knew she meant it. She'd called him "sir."

He opened his eyes and bought his mouth to Anya's. She opened herself up to his kiss, to his tongue, to his lips. Her mouth tasted as sweet and intoxicating as a dessert wine.

Daniel willed himself to slow down and think. He had condoms, lube...what he needed was a little self-control here or he'd rip her open. Before opening his eyes, Daniel took deep breaths. He hadn't been this aroused in years. Not with Irina, not with Eleanor, not since Maggie. He had to stay calm. He had to be in control. Especially since she was sacrificing her chance to save her siblings by sleeping with him.

He wanted her but he wanted to take care of her, too. Her and her family.

"Any price," he whispered into her mouth. "I'll pay it."

"What?"

He smiled against her lips. "If I take your virginity you won't be in the auction. I'll pay you whatever you want for it."

Anya tried to pull her hands away from him. He didn't let go.

"Pay me?"

Something in her voice warned him he'd said the wrong thing...or the right thing the wrong way.

"I didn't mean it like that. Only—"

Anya tried pulling away again.

"Anya, stop. Please listen. You're worried about money, about your brothers and—"

"You think I want to give myself to you for money?"

"No. But you were in the auction for money. And I know you want money and God knows I have more of it than anyone needs. I just meant I'd pay you—"

"Leonard."

Daniel almost didn't understand what she said. But the look in her eyes told him exactly what she meant.

He released her immediately and Anya sat up and pulled her knees tight to her chest in a sudden display of modesty.

"My dress," she said, her voice hollow and cold. "Please. And please put your clothes on, too."

Daniel moved off the bed and picked up her sodden dress from the floor.

Anya wouldn't even look at him.

He handed her the dress and she held it to her chest and made no move to put it on. Then he realized she was waiting for him to leave, to turn his back. Just two minutes ago she'd been completely naked underneath him, her legs open wide, her body wet and waiting for him...now she'd pulled tight into herself, shut down, pushed him away.

Daniel walked into the bathroom and found his pants. As he pulled them on, he berated himself for saying, yet again, exactly the wrong thing to Anya. He'd only meant to help her, to comfort her, to take some of the pressure off of her. That was the only reason he'd offered to pay her. He had to make her understand.

"Anya!" Daniel ran from of the bathroom and found his bed wet and empty. Calling her name again he raced to the living room, tracing her wet footprints. Throwing the front door open, he saw the elevator at the end of hall closing. Had he been able to fly he still wouldn't have made it there in time to keep it from closing. But that didn't stop him from trying.

A few feet from the elevator he called Anya's name again. All she had to do was reach out and hit the Door Open button. But she had her arms wrapped tight around herself. She looked broken and beautiful, her dress wet with bathwater, her face wet with tears.

"Anya...please stay."

"I hate you."

The door shut in his face. And she was gone. And he knew chasing after her right now would only make things worse.

Daniel returned to his apartment and couldn't even look at the wet mess in the bathroom, on his bed. He stayed in the living room all night, stretched out on the couch, going over every perfect moment with Anya in his head.

The second he had her in his arms, it felt like he finally knew why he had arms. The second he kissed her he understood why he had lips. The peaceful contentment in her eyes as she knelt at his feet made him understand why he'd been born to dominate in the bedroom. And when she lay beneath him in his bed, he understood for the first time why Eleanor had let him go—because he didn't belong with her.

He belonged with Anya.

There'd even been a moment tonight—fleeting, the span of a skipped heartbeat—when he'd thought, "She's the one. She's the one I'm going to marry someday. She's the one Maggie wants for me, why she left me that note, why I found it today..."

He'd died when Maggie died and Eleanor brought him back to life. And now that he was alive, he knew exactly who he wanted on stage with him for Daniel Part Two. Anya.

That she'd lied to come see him, and had been willing to give up so much money to give her virginity to him instead of at the auction meant only one thing—she was falling in love with him, too.

And he'd fucked it up completely.

He barely slept that night. Or the next. He called Anya every day and received no answer. He stopped by Signore Vitale's and was told time and time again she was working at another shop—and no, Daniel couldn't have the address of it. Even Kingsley was of no help.

"She told me she wants to be in the auction, *mon ami*. And she told me to keep you away from her."

"When did you start taking orders from sub-missives?" Daniel had demanded of Kingsley.

"Hell hath no fury like a woman scorned," Kingsley said, "and I do take orders from furies."

Daniel spent that night fantasizing of elaborate ways of killing Kingsley. By morning he'd decided on the guillotine. Fitting for a Frenchman. And a traitor.

Three days passed without Daniel hearing a word from Anya or even being able to see her. And during those three days apart from her, he realized he'd give every penny he had just to kiss her again. That's all. Just a kiss. Less than a kiss. He'd give every cent he had to know she was safe and wouldn't be giving her body to a dangerous stranger.

Every last cent.

That thought followed him to bed the night before Kingsley's auction. It lay with him on his pillow and whispered to him until dawn.

And when he woke up the following morning, he knew exactly what he had to do.

He picked up the phone and called Eleanor.

————

"YOU'RE AN IDIOT. You realize that, right?"

Daniel sighed and sank back into his leather sofa. "Yes, I realize that. I also realized that when you told me the same thing five minutes ago. This verbal abuse is well-deserved, Elle, but not particularly helpful."

Eleanor stopped pacing the length of his living room rug and turned to face him.

"Can you at least explain to me why, at the most intensely vulnerable moment of Anya's life, you decided to offer her money for her virginity? Can you do that for me, Daniel? I'm begging you to do that for me. If I woke up to find a crop circle in my bedroom, I would be less curious about the origin of that than I am about why the hell someone as intelligent as you would do something that mind-blowingly stupid. Jesus, Mary and Joseph, I swear..."

Crossing herself dramatically, Eleanor collapsed and lay like a murder victim in the center of the floor. With one finger she started outlining her body, etching a makeshift chalk outline in the pile of the rug.

"I wasn't thinking with my head at the time. Sorry. Anya's in the auction to make money so she could get her brothers and sisters out from under her father's thumb. I just wanted her to know that if she slept with me, she wouldn't have to worry about the money. I would take care of her. She didn't have to worry about anything—money or otherwise. That's all I was trying to say."

The corpse of Eleanor raised her head and stared at him.

"And you just couldn't say it just like that? You couldn't say, 'Don't worry about anything. I will take care of you'? Trust me, that's hot. I'm speaking as a woman who is constantly broke and if a guy told me he'd take care of me, I'd appreciate it. Actually, I probably should have thought of that before falling in love with a man under a vow of poverty. If I fuck you again, will you pay off my student loans?"

Daniel glared at her.

She shrugged. "Worth a shot."

Daniel rubbed his forehead as he re-imagined that moment with Anya on his bed:

Don't worry about anything, Anya. I'll take care of you... And maybe she'd ask him what he meant by that, and he could have said, *I want you but not just in my bed and not just tonight. I want you in my life. And I want kids, lots of them, and you come with five of them. I'll take them all because I have big empty house in the country that you and all your brothers and sisters are welcome to. If you want children of your own we can have them and if not, that's fine. Let me own you, all of you, and you will never have to worry about anything ever again...*

If he had said that, what he really meant, she would have stayed all night. And maybe even forever.

"Am I insane for thinking I could fall in love with her?" Daniel asked.

"No. But you are insane for fucking it up so badly."

"I do that a lot."

She gave him a look. Pursed lips. Pure disapproval.

"Stop with the self-pity," she said. "You didn't fuck anything up with me. I was already in love with someone else when we met. And you didn't fuck anything up with Maggie, and you know she'd say the same thing."

Daniel sighed again. "She would, yeah. She even...she left me a note telling me to get married again because I was such a good husband to her."

"See?"

"And yet...I'm fucked."

"Well and truly fucked, Danny Boy. Question is —how are we going to get you un-fucked?"

Daniel slid from the couch to the floor and lay down beside Eleanor. "I think I have an idea."

"Please don't tell me you're going to buy her at the auction tonight."

"I'm going to buy her at the auction tonight."

"You can't."

"Why not? Bad idea?"

"Impossible idea. See?"

Eleanor rolled over and grabbed her bag. Digging through it she tossed out books and pens and notebooks, a small brown plush animal dinosaur, a map of Belgium, a package of birth control pills, a pair of handcuffs, a set of rosary beads, and finally some kind of folded card.

"Here." She gave him the paper. "It's the auction program for the night. Look under the submissive listings—they're the ones on the left."

Daniel studied the cover of the program. The

heavy black paper was embossed with gold ink. "The 8th Annual King's Trust Charity Auction." *King's Trust.* Cute, Kingsley. Very classy.

Daniel opened the program. As was customary, the submissives were auctioned off first—three women and two men. After intermission, it was the dominants' turn—two women and two men, including Daniel.

True to form, Kingsley had made sure everything looked respectable and above-board. The program boasted that the winners would be allowed an evening on the town with their prize—all expenses included in the winning bid. Daniel knew what the phrase "all expenses included" was code for.

Winner takes all. BDSM, sex, and BDSM sex.

Daniel scanned the listings and found Anya as the last item on the submissive side of the program. Next to her name written in elegant calligraphy were the words "Grand Prize – Take Anya on her First Date Ever." Daniel's stomach churned at the words "First Date." Code for "still a virgin." An animalistic possessiveness reared up in him. Anyone who dared bid on Anya would run the risk of the world's most dangerously infatuated librarian dominant tearing him apart limb from limb.

"Check out the disclaimer," Eleanor said.

At the bottom of the program it read, *Auction prizes are not allowed to bid.*

"I was afraid of that," he said. "She must have

told Kingsley to keep me out of the bidding."

Eleanor shook her head as she threw her flotsam back into her bag. "Did I mention you're an idiot and this entire mess was preventable if you'd been thinking with your actual head?"

"Does your owner let you talk to him like this?"

"The first words out of my mouth when I met him were 'You're an idiot.' It was love at first slight."

At that Daniel could only laugh miserably as he gazed up at the ceiling.

"So Plan B?" Eleanor asked.

Plan B. Daniel had hoped it wouldn't come to this. He'd fucked things up badly enough with Anya that he feared any sort of subterfuge on his part would only make it worse. But it wasn't about having her anymore or taking her virginity—not that it had ever been about that. He had to keep her safe. Even if she ended up hating him and never speaking to him again...it didn't matter. It wasn't about him and his happiness. Only Anya.

He turned his head and looked at Eleanor lying next to him on the floor. She was such a beautiful woman with her black hair and green-black eyes, her full breasts and fuller lips, her intelligence, her wicked wit, and her untamable heart. And for the first time in a year and a half, he didn't even remotely want her.

She raised her eyebrow at him and waited.

"You aren't in the auction, are you?"

Eleanor stared at him. "God, you're an idiot."

10

At seven that night, Daniel did something he hadn't done in years—he stood in front of a mirror wearing a suit and tying a tie. He'd foregone ties ever since Maggie's funeral as he couldn't put one on without remembering that day. But tonight's auction called for formal attire. So on went an old suit of his Maggie had bought for him. It was Armani, a very nice suit, but it didn't fit him quite right anymore. The trousers were too baggy, the jacket too tight on his shoulders. Kingsley would throw a fit but Daniel didn't care.

He'd just finished tying his tie when he heard a knock on the door. Daniel wondered who it could be at this hour. Eleanor had agreed to his plan—after calling him an idiot a few more times—but said she would have to meet him at Kingsley's where the auction would be held. He hoped Anya might have had a sudden change of heart but he knew better than to dream that big.

Opening the door he saw a small elderly man standing out in the hallway with a black garment bag.

"Signore Vitale?"

"Signore Caldwell. Your suit is ready."

"My suit? Right, of course." Daniel had almost forgotten he'd been fitted for a new wardrobe. He simply assumed Anya would have put anything of his at the very bottom of her to do list. Or burnt it.

Daniel took the garment bag from Signore Vitale. "Thank you for bringing it to me. I didn't realize you delivered."

"I usually don't. I leave that to my assistant." Signore Vitale smiled sadly at him. "She politely declined."

Daniel's heart sank. "I'm not surprised."

Signore Vitale nodded at the garment bag. "Go. Try it on."

"Of course. Please come in."

Daniel left Signore Vitale in his living room while he went back to his bedroom and stripped out of his clothes. He unzipped the garment bag and found an exquisite three-piece suit inside—black with silver pinstripes. Although distinctly modern it had a retro 1940s cut to it. All he needed was a fedora to look like he'd just stepped out of a Humphrey Bogart movie.

Once dressed, Daniel stared at his reflection in the mirror. He'd never really seen what women found so compelling about him—not terribly tall and certainly not pretty. But tonight in this suit he looked...

"Damn," was all Daniel could say.

He went into the living room and found Signore Vitale waiting by the windows.

"Perfect fit," Daniel said. More than perfect, the suit fit like his own skin.

"My assistant, she does amazing work. Far better than mine even when I was a young man. I've never seen her work so hard on one piece before. Even last night she stayed late at the shop picking out the perfect buttons."

Daniel's stomach clenched at the thought of Anya working late sewing his suit by hand. "Anya did all the work?"

"Every single stitch. Seemed to be a labor of love for her. Such a talent. I'll miss her."

"Miss her?"

Signore Vitale nodded. "She put in her notice. She's moving back to Quebec to be with her family again."

Be with her family again? Or to run away from him and how much he had hurt her? If Anya went back to Quebec, he knew she would never leave again. She'd become a mother to her siblings and give up her whole life taking care of them. Daniel couldn't let that happen.

"When's her last day?"

"It was yesterday. She's going back tomorrow."

"Tomorrow?" Auction tonight, leaving tomorrow... "That's not going to happen. I'll keep her here if I have to tie her down."

"Something tells me she might enjoy that."

Daniel smiled. "Send me the bill. I have to go."

"No bill. Anya paid for it."

Guilt speared his heart like a knife. Damn stubborn girl. If she kept this up, he'd be forced to ask her to marry him.

"Send the bill anyway. Thank you for bringing this to me. Now you'll have to excuse me. I'm going to go buy your assistant."

Signore Vitale shook his head. "I hope you are as rich as Croesus then. That girl is priceless."

"Worth every penny."

Daniel took a cab to Kingsley's. Limousines and Rolls Royces, Caddies and black Lincolns came and went, dropping off their well-heeled passengers. Daniel pushed past an actress he vaguely recognized and into the house just as Eleanor skipped down the main stairway toward him. He couldn't help but smile at her. At formal events in Kingsley's world, all the submissives were expected to wear white. Eleanor had on a white Regency style gown with a bow in the front that fell all the way to the hem. Her long black hair was pinned up in curls and ringlets. And around her neck she wore her white collar that looked merely like a choker. She looked as if she'd stepped out of the pages of a Jane Austen novel.

"Daniel, you look so fucking hot, I'd suck you off right now if we weren't in public."

"And Jane Austen spins in her grave. You look lovely."

"Thank you. So the plan..."

"Is idiotic, as you said. But it's the only one I have. Can I trust you to go through with it?"

Eleanor batted her dark eyelashes at him. "You know I'll do anything to get in trouble with Blondie."

"Is he here?" Daniel asked.

"Of course he is. Maybe we should get him to bid for you instead of me. It's all kinksters here tonight. Nobody would ever bid against him."

"I can believe that. No offense but I trust you more than I trust him."

"That's very sweet, Daniel, but I just stole your wallet."

Eleanor held up his wallet.

Daniel rolled his eyes and took it back from her. "Come on," he said.

The two of them mounted the stairs and headed up to the top floor. Kingsley had a glass-enclosed rooftop garden and as usual the auction would take place there, illuminated both by candlelight and city-light.

The auction had just begun by the time they arrived. Eleanor waited at his side under an orange tree. On the opposite side of the garden, Eleanor's owner stood next to Kingsley and watched them both intently.

"Are you really going to get into trouble for helping me?" Daniel whispered to Eleanor.

"Well, you're not his favorite person, but I think I'll come out of it with my head still attached to my body."

"You sure you want to go through with it?"

"Daniel." She looked up at him and grinned. "Do you even have to ask?"

He smiled back. "I'm glad you dumped me. You terrify me."

"You say the sweetest things."

Boisterous applause and wolf-whistling erupted as Kingsley came to stand on the small stage at the center of the crowd. Daniel barely heard a word of Kingsley's welcome speech and his thank you's to everyone for helping support his King's Trust charity with their bids tonight.

"I love you, Kingsley," a woman shouted out in the middle of his speech.

"Your taste is impeccable," he replied without missing a beat. "See me after the auction."

The first submissive took the stage and the auctioneer, a handsome older gentleman with silver hair, began the bidding.

"Oh, hello there," Eleanor purred.

"Are you lusting after the auctioneer?" Daniel whispered.

"No, him." She nodded toward the person on the stage—a tall young man who looked about twenty. He had tan skin that made his blue eyes look even brighter. His shaggy dark brown hair fell across his forehead and he nervously swiped it to the side.

"Buy him for me," Eleanor begged, turning her pouting face up to him.

Daniel glanced down at the auction program— Antonio, age twenty. Beside his name was a tiny, lower-case S.

"He's a submissive, Elle. Not your type."

Eleanor's eyes narrowed at the young man and for a moment she looked genuinely dangerous, almost predatory. "Oh. Right. Not my type."

She didn't sound the least bit disappointed.

The submissive sold to a man in the audience for an impressive ninety thousand dollars. Daniel could only imagine what the young man would have to submit to that night to justify that ninety grand.

The auction continued and the next three submissives sold between a hundred and a hundred and fifty thousand dollars.

"Wow. Big spenders tonight," Eleanor said. "This is more than they made last year in the entire auction. Hope you're ready to pay up."

"I'm ready," Daniel said.

"You do realize this might not work, right?" Eleanor asked, looking at him with genuine concern in her green-black eyes. "Anya might still hate you."

He nodded. "I'm not buying her to win her forgiveness. I just want her to be safe."

Eleanor rose up on her tip-toes and kissed him on the cheek. "She's an idiot, too, if she doesn't love you back."

"You didn't love me back."

"I'm an idiot. Now shush. It's starting."

Kingsley came back to the stage and introduced their last prize before the intermission. Daniel's hands went numb and his heart fluttered painfully as Anya stepped onto the stage and clung to Kingsley's hand.

"My God..." Daniel breathed. He'd never seen a more beautiful woman in his life. Anya wore a simple gown of pure white. Two small braids formed a crown around her head like a halo while the rest of her long red-black hair fell in waves down her back. On her face she wore a tight smile and a look of sadness tinged with fear in her eyes.

Kingsley kissed the back of her hand, whispered something in her ear, and left the stage.

Daniel's heart pounded ferociously in his chest. The auctioneer took the stage again and began the bidding.

"Let's begin the bidding at fifty thousand dollars."

"What do you want me to bid?" Eleanor asked in a whisper.

"What was the winning bid last time for the grand prize?"

"A lot."

One man in the crowd bid the fifty. Another man bid sixty-nine thousand, which led to a round of laughter from the crowd. Daniel memorized that bidder's face so he could find it and break it later. Meanwhile Anya waited on the stage, doing her best impression of a statue.

Yet another man bid ninety-thousand.

Then a gasp rippled through the crowd.

Someone had just bid two-hundred thousand dollars. But not just any someone.

"Holy fuck..." Eleanor breathed. "Blondie just on bid on Anya."

She clasped her hand over her mouth in obvious shock.

Daniel stared across the crowd and found Eleanor's owner smiling dangerously at him. No, not smiling. Smirking. And Daniel saw a message in that smirk, a message that read, *You had mine. Now I'll have yours.*

Kingsley stood next to him, holding a checkbook in his hand.

"Son of a bitch," Daniel said. "What the hell is Søren doing, bidding on Anya?"

"Punishing you for trying to steal me? Mindfuck? Decided to dump me and this is how he's telling me? All of the above?"

"Any other bids?" The auctioneer gazed around the crowd.

"I can't let you bid for me," Daniel said. "Not against your owner."

"He's making me pick again," she said. "You or him."

"Fuck," Daniel breathed.

"Do you love her?" Eleanor asked.

"I want to. But I—"

"It's okay," she said with a smile. "You can pick her over me. I promise."

Daniel wrenched his eyes from Eleanor's handsome smirking owner and looked at Anya. He'd warned her a sadist might bid on her and clearly, from the look of abject terror on her face, she knew exactly who that sadist was. *The* sadist.

"How much do you want me to bid?" Eleanor asked.

"If there are no further bids," the auctioneer said.

"Hurry, Daniel."

"He'll be furious at you."

"He's cute when he's mad. Winning bid last time was two-hundred and fifty-six thousand," she reminded him. She didn't need to remind him. He knew the exact amount. "So...?"

"Bid this," Daniel said and handed her a cashier's check.

It was the same amount *Le Grand Prix* had gone for last year, multiplied by ten.

———

ELEANOR RAISED her hand and in a clear strong voice called out, "Two million five hundred and sixty thousand dollars."

The entire assembly gasped again.

"Did I do that right?" Eleanor whispered. "I hope I did that right. I'm shit at math."

"Madam?" the auctioneer said as he turned to her. "Are you quite sure?"

Eleanor nodded. "Oh, hell yes," she said toward Anya. "I'd hit that."

From across the room Eleanor's owner's smirk turned into a furious steely-eyed glare.

"He's going to kill you, isn't he?" Daniel asked.

"Probably. Ask me if I care."

From the stage the auctioneer announced, "Going once...going twice...sold to the young woman in the white dress who would hit that."

Eleanor ran to the stage, took Anya by the hand, and dragged her toward Daniel.

"Don't worry," Eleanor was saying to Anya as she brought the girl to him. "I won't make you put out. Unless you just really want to. Here's the money man. I bought you but he's my backer. See?"

"Pen?" Daniel handed Eleanor an ink pen.

"Give me a second...I want to enjoy this." Eleanor held onto the check, gazing at it adoringly for a moment and kissing it with a dramatic flourish. Then, with a sigh, she said, "Okay. I'm at peace."

She signed the check over to Anya. "Was nice while it lasted. Talk to Daniel. I need to go get flogged right now."

With a wink, Eleanor ran off to her owner. They disappeared into Kingsley's house and were gone.

Anya turned to him, and Daniel raised his hand.

"Let me speak. Please," he said and Anya closed her mouth. "I'm an idiot. I said exactly the opposite of what I meant to say that night. All I meant was...I want you in my life. I want to take care of you. And all your brothers and sisters. I'll take care of them like they were my own family. Even Leonard. I'm sorry for ruining things. Truly sorry."

Anya smiled a little but he didn't let her speak.

"Eleanor bought you, not me. You don't owe me—or anyone—anything. I'm asking nothing of you but forgiveness. Anyway, you look beautiful tonight. You always look beautiful. And...no, that's everything. I'm done making an ass of myself now."

He stood there in silence and waited. Anya looked everywhere but up at him.

Finally she opened her mouth.

"I forgive you," she said before turning on her heel and walking away into Kingsley's house and out of his life.

11

He closed his eyes and leaned back against the trunk of the orange tree. All of his hopes for Anya...all of his dreams for them...he let them go. Because they were so low on his priority list compared to her safety that he couldn't even begin to be sad yet. He knew he would be, tomorrow perhaps, and then every day of his life after. But she wouldn't be giving her body to a stranger tonight, so he considered his idiotic plan a rousing success.

The crowd stood up and mingled amongst each other. Waiters came bearing wine and champagne. Kingsley strolled over to him and looked him up and down.

"Your suit," Kingsley said.

"Yes?"

"It's an improvement."

Daniel laughed coldly. "Anya made it. Even paid for it herself."

"Her way of serving you your own testicles on a platter."

"Feels like it. I won her, Kingsley. And I lost her. Then I won her again. And I lost her again. I just keep losing. Know any florists still open? I'll bring her lilies. Two million five hundred and sixty thousand dollars' worth of lilies. Think that would work?"

"Poor Daniel." Kingsley clicked his tongue like an obnoxious French hen. "I spent a weekend in Monte Carlo not that long ago. I saw a man who kept losing and losing and losing...but finally he stopped losing. Do you know why he finally stopped losing?"

Daniel shook his head.

Kingsley smiled. "He stopped the playing the game."

"Whose side are you on?"

"Mine, always."

Kingsley patted his cheek condescendingly and strolled off.

"It's Mass-ah-CHEW-setts," Daniel called after him.

"Don't forget, you're up next on the block," Kingsley called back, while Daniel mentally served Kingsley his own testicles on a platter. He hated to admit the Frenchman might have a point. He hated to admit it...so he wouldn't admit it. Not out loud, anyway.

Intermission ended and the auctioneer took the stage again. The crowd seemed even more excited about the second half of the auction than the first half. Daniel supposed seeing the Underground's most infamous dominants on display like submissives usually were provided a bit of amusement along with the shock value. Kingsley's paid doms cultivated an air of mystery and danger about them. Kingsley's does were not summoned, not for any amount of money. They saw clients at their leisure only. One simply signed up on the waiting list and waited to be summoned. And paid through the nose for the privilege.

Daniel, of course, knew he had no such air of power or mystery. As dominants went he wasn't particularly noteworthy, at least not in his own mind. If Daniel brought in ten grand on the auction block, he'd be surprised. Not that he cared. He just wanted it over with. He'd already decided to write a check to whomever bought a night with him, for the exact amount they'd paid. That way he'd keep his promise to Kingsley, the charity would get its money, and no one would lose out. Also, most importantly, he wouldn't have to touch anyone who wasn't Anya.

The auctioneer introduced him, and with a sigh Daniel stepped forward. Once up there he discovered he could barely see past the blazing candles that decorated the stage. He heard laughter and applause. A woman's voice, gilded with a distinct Russian accent, proclaimed, "If anyone bids against me, they're getting a flogging." Someone set off another round of tittering by helpfully reminding her that in this crowd, that wasn't much of a threat.

Bidding began at ten thousand dollars and quickly shot up to fifty. Fifty thousand dollars. For him? What madwoman in the crowd would pay fifty thousand dollars for one night with him? Had to be Irina. She had made it very clear she wanted to see him again after their one torrid afternoon together.

At eighty thousand dollars the bidding stalled. Well, that was about ten times as much as he'd expected anyone would bid for him. He should be flattered. Instead he felt nothing but empty, lonely.

"Any other bids?" the auctioneer called out. There was no answer. "Going once...going twice..."

"Two-million, five-hundred and sixty-thousand *dollarz*," came a voice from the crowd.

Daniel's ears perked up.

Dollarz?

With a z?

Anya.

And then Daniel heard the most beautiful word he'd ever heard in his entire life.

"Sold."

———

HE RACED off the stage and found Anya waiting for him under the orange tree.

"Anya? What are you—"

She held up her hand. "My turn to talk," she

said. "You hurt me more than anyone has ever hurt me in my entire life that night."

Daniel started to speak and she clapped her hand over his mouth.

"My. Turn."

Daniel nodded and let her go on.

"But I know now that I overreacted," she said. "I do that sometimes. You said that you meant to say you wanted to take care of me, that you even want to take care of my brothers and sisters."

She shook her head, and he saw tears gathering at the corners of those beautiful amber eyes.

Anya continued, "I think you are *fou*...crazy. But I'm *fou,* too, because I want all of that...and I want it with you."

She paused and took a breath. She blinked and the tears raced down her face.

"I want to be yours," she said. "I want to belong to you...sir."

It took a few seconds for Daniel's brain to catch up with his heart. And then a second or two more for his mouth to catch up with his brain.

"I only have one thing to say to you," he said. "What are your orders, Mistress?"

He caressed her cheek and she smiled into his hand.

"Orders?" she asked.

"You bought me. You own me. At least tonight. Tomorrow and after, I'll own you."

"I have an order," she said. "One order—make love to me."

Daniel had never been so happy to follow an order in his life—but he was still the dominant here, even though he knew at this moment and forever, Anya now owned him, too.

He cleared his throat pointedly. "What was that?"

Anya grinned through her tears. "Please make love to me...sir."

"Better. And yes, right now."

He grabbed her wrist and dragged her bodily from the rooftop garden. He just needed a room, any room. Any room with a bed. Forget the bed, he'd take a floor, a desk, a wall.

Anya's pulse raced wildly against his hand as he pulled her down the hall. Sounds of agony and ecstasy, sometimes separate, sometimes mixed, echoed out from behind many of the closed doors.

Only the room at the very end of the hall seemed to be free of ongoing orgies. Daniel pushed open the door and found a beautiful red-headed goddess lounging across the bed in one of Kingsley's shirts.

"Out," Daniel ordered.

"But—"

"Out. Now."

The girl rolled off the bed, grabbed her clothes, and with a look of pure hatred at him and Anya, left them alone.

Daniel slammed the door behind her, locked it, and pushed Anya up against the wall with more force than was necessary.

"You're not leaving this room a virgin." Daniel spoke the words before pressing his lips to the side of her neck, just under her ear.

"*Monsieur's* room?" Anya wrapped her arms around his shoulders and clung to him. He slipped a hand under her dress, hooked her leg around his waist, and gripped her thigh. "He won't mind?"

"He'll mind, especially since I kicked his date out. But Kingsley can kiss my ass. Don't tell him I said that. He might take it literally."

Anya started to laugh but he cut her off with a kiss to her lips so hungry he thought it might consume them both. As he kissed her, Daniel pressed his hips into hers and was gratified to feel her press back.

Daniel pulled her away from the wall and slid the straps of her dress off her shoulders and down her arms. Shoving the dress down her body, he hooked his thumbs into her white panties and brought them down to the floor as well. Now Anya stood in front of him naked but for her shoes and the halo of her hair.

She was exquisite. Her breasts were a perfect handful, her nipples dark pink and getting redder as he gazed on them. Her soft stomach quivered as she breathed nervously. She was shaved bare and his mouth watered at the thought of licking that smooth naked mound down to her clitoris, her labia and even inside of her.

"Nice shoes," Daniel said.

"They're Mary Janes. Very comfortable."

"I'm sure they'll feel quite comfortable on my back."

At that Anya blushed, just as he'd wanted her to. He lifted her in his arms and laid her across Kingsley's massive bed. Kingsley might have had a virgin in his bed before—Daniel would put nothing past that man—but he knew never before had a woman so beautiful graced these sheets. And she was his, all his.

Anya settled against the sheets of Kingsley's rather infamous big red bed. Daniel pulled off his jacket and tossed it over the back of the chair. Anya rolled up to sitting as he started on the buttons of his vest.

"Let me," she said. "Please, sir."

Smiling, Daniel dropped his hands to his sides.

With shaking hands, Anya unbuttoned the vest and pushed it off his shoulders. She let it fall to the floor.

"The floor?" Daniel raised an eyebrow at her. "This is my favorite suit, you know. It shouldn't end up on the floor."

"As I was making it," she whispered as she started on the buttons of his shirt, "I couldn't help but imagine it on the floor by the bed, sir. I wanted to hate you. I did hate you. But I only hated you, because I loved you."

"If that's how you hate me, then hate me for the rest of your life."

Daniel caressed her naked back as she unbuttoned his shirt and pulled it out of his suit trousers. But she didn't stop there. She opened his pants, slipped her hands inside, and wrapped her fingers around him.

"Bad idea," he whispered in her ear.

Anya started to pull away but he grabbed both her wrists. "Just because it's a bad idea doesn't mean you're allowed to stop."

Laughing softly, Anya leaned her head against his chest. Daniel wrapped an arm around her as she kept exploring him with her fingers.

"Are you on birth control?" he whispered as he caressed her spine from the nape of her neck down to the base and up again. "Or do I need—"

"Please," she said, looking up at him. "I've been on it for three months. And I want nothing between us, sir."

"Me neither. Never again."

Anya nodded, seemingly unable to speak. She looked down and watched herself touching him. At first her fingers moved tentatively, but she grew bolder with each stroke and his shuddering breaths that followed. He heard her mumble something.

"Louder and in English," he ordered.

When Anya turned her face up to him, he saw she was blushing. "I said I can't imagine how we'll fit all of that inside me."

Daniel cupped her chin and kissed her lips "Very carefully. Lay down."

Obediently, Anya rolled onto her back. Her hands clenched nervously at the red sheets underneath her shivering body. He lifted her leg and pressed a kiss onto the sensitive skin of her ankle, right above the strap of her white Mary Jane.

With torturous slowness he kissed his way up the inside of her leg, lingering at her knee...then lingering even longer at the inside of her thigh. He felt her whole body stiffen as he kissed even higher. Gently, he bit her hips and the soft skin at the base of her stomach before dipping his head lower. Pressing her legs wide, he licked her bare labia and sucked lightly on her clitoris.

"Sir—" She gasped in shock, and he sensed she wanted to scoot away. With an iron grip he clamped both hands on her hips and held her in place.

Using his elbows, he pried her resisting thighs open even wider. Now he remembered why he'd avoided virgins in the past—the nervousness, the shyness, the fear of the unknown threatening to overshadow the moment's pleasures. But with Anya he felt the privilege of being her first lover, of teaching her, training her. Once she learned how to give herself to him sexually, he'd teach her to submit to him in other ways— submit to pain, to darker pleasures, to every delicious sensation and temptation he could devise for her.

"Stop hiding from me," he said, digging his fingers into her soft skin hard enough he knew she'd have finger shaped bruises on her thighs tomorrow. Good. The sooner she learned the consequences of trying to keep her body from him, the better. "Relax."

Anya whimpered in the back of her throat and relaxed her legs.

"Better. Now behave. You might actually enjoy this."

Once again Daniel brought his lips to Anya's clitoris and gently sucked on it. As he made love to her with his mouth, he brought two fingers to her body and slowly started to work them into her tight vagina.

She stiffened as before but didn't attempt to close her legs. Good girl. She could be taught. Slowly, he pushed into her, nearly groaning aloud as her wet warmth surrounded his fingers.

Carefully he spread his fingers apart inside her, hoping to open up her tight passage for him. But she tasted so good, so tart and sweet and womanly, that he almost forgot this act wasn't the sole reason they'd stolen Kingsley's room. Through the haze of his own desire Daniel heard Anya starting to enjoy his lips and tongue on her. She whimpered and gasped, then lifted her hips to push herself harder against his mouth.

Daniel took that and the wet heat inside her as a sign that she was as ready as she could be for him. He pulled away and covered her body with his own. Immediately Anya wrapped her legs around his naked back. The heels of her shoes cut into his skin, a delicious little agony.

He gathered her delicate wrists in one hand

and pressed them over her head. The veil of contented submission had fallen across her eyes again. She looked calm, peaceful, almost drowsy with lust. He wanted her just like that when he entered her. A thousand things went through his mind that he wanted to say to her at that moment. But for her own sake he said nothing, merely let her relax into subspace, as he opened her up wide with his fingertips and started to push inside.

Anya's half-closed eyes flew open wide and she let out a cry of obvious agony. With a groan of frustration Daniel pulled back and away from her.

"*Non,* sir. Please." Anya rolled up and wrapped her arms around her knees looking nervous as a child. "I'm sorry. Please don't stop."

"Don't apologize for being in pain. And a gun to my head wouldn't stop me now."

Daniel knelt down and pulled a silver case out from under Kingsley's bed. The other cases called to him but he knew tonight was not the night to introduce Anya to the crop or the flogger. He snapped open the lid and found exactly what he wanted. Anya had confessed her need to be restrained during sex. But flat on her back underneath him, she would have no chance to control the pain of penetration.

Daniel stood up and Anya's eyes went wide as she saw the handcuffs. He raised his chin, stared down at her, and spun the silver cuffs in his hand —a little trick that always raised Maggie's heart rate. It seemed to have a similar effect on Anya.

"By the headboard," he said. "Go."

Anya crawled to the head of the bed. That body of hers...on her hands and knees, crawling. Soon he would teach her the beauty of crawling for him.

Daniel shed the rest of his clothes and crawled across the bed to meet her. He sat with his back to the headboard and gripped Anya by the waist. She laughed a little as he lifted her onto his lap.

"Right hand."

Anya raised her arm and gave her hand to him. He kissed the pulse point on her wrist before slapping the cuffs on her. Before she could even think of protesting he hooked the handcuffs through the metal bar on Kingsley's headboard, grabbed Anya's left wrist and cuffed it, too. Now she sat on his thighs in front of him, handcuffed to the bed. He might be imprisoned by her arms at each side of his head but he knew of no prison he'd rather spend his whole life inside.

"Beautiful...the most beautiful *Québécoise* in the world," he said, tracing the outline of her body with his hands. Groaning, Anya's head fell back as Daniel took her by the waist. He raised her nipples to his lips and sucked lightly on them. Once more he pushed two fingers inside her. He opened his fingers wide while with his other hand he guided the tip to her wet entrance.

"I'm so ashamed," she whispered as she arched her back pushing her breasts into his chest.

"Of what?"

"I'm in love...with a Canadian."

"Imagine how I feel," Daniel said as he kissed her chest, right over her heart. "I'm about to make love to Celine Dion."

She laughed and he laughed and when they were done laughing, they kissed. And when they were done kissing, Daniel guided Anya to his cock and held her hips as she lowered herself onto him. Their eyes locked and he said nothing, did nothing but let her own courage and body weight bring her down onto him.

"Go as slow as you need to. Breathe."

Nodding she closed her eyes and breathed through her nose in short bursts. She took an inch, stopped to breathe, took another inch, breathed again.

"I'm sorry," she said again. "It hurts much less this way. But it's still..."

Daniel cupped her face and kissed her lips. "You're doing fine, Anya."

"I want...I want all of you. Please...help me, sir."

Sliding his hands down her body, Daniel decided quicker might be better. He wrapped his fingers around her hips and held her steady. Once more he met her scared, wide amber eyes. Then he pushed up and into her, taking her virginity with one thrust.

Anya cried out and buried her head in the crook of his neck. Daniel wrapped his arms around her and held her close. For a torturous minute he did nothing but let her whimper and struggle and cry. Being so deep inside her without moving nearly killed him. But her pain muted his desire and allowed him to keep whispering words of comfort and love to her.

He slipped a hand between their bodies and rubbed her clitoris. At first she flinched from obvious pain. But he lightened his touch, caressed her even more gently, and when she whimpered again, he could tell it was from pleasure.

"Try moving," he said as he increased the pressure on her.

Anya obediently began careful undulations of her hips. Daniel had to swallow a groan of pleasure. He didn't want her hurting herself by trying to please him.

"Better?" he asked when the movements grew wider and her body seemed to relax.

"It feels..." she began and stopped. "It feels like you belong inside me."

Daniel's heart tightened in his chest. "That's because I do."

His fingers moved faster, making tight circles to match the circles of her swaying hips. Turning his head, he kissed the inside of her arm that encircled him and nibbled on the soft flesh at the inside of her elbows. He couldn't resist one hard bite that would leave a bruise on her forearm. Someday soon he'd leave her body covered with welts and bruises.

Anya gasped and flinched and Daniel felt her

inner muscles flutter around him. He kept circling her clitoris, kept holding back his own needs as Anya kept moving her hips on him, taking him deeper and deeper with every push against him.

"You have my permission to come whenever you can," Daniel said, wanting to start training her to only orgasm when he allowed it. He'd wait a few weeks before bringing the rougher toys out. But discipline began tonight.

Daniel's left hand ran all over her body while his right hand continued to tease her. When his hand brushed her neck Anya took a hard breath. He wrapped his fingers around her throat and held her neck lightly. It seemed to be exactly what she needed. Anya pulled hard against the handcuffs as she pumped her hips into him. What little restraint Daniel had left disappeared as she released a loud throaty cry. Both hands grabbed her soft bottom with bruising force as he pushed up hard and came inside her.

Together they breathed through the climax, half-panting, half-laughing at their loss of control.

Daniel kissed Anya's lips, her forehead, her cheek, her neck. "Good girl," he whispered. "Did you enjoy that?"

She nodded. "Again?"

Daniel brushed the hair off her forehead. "I'm thirty-eight. Give me minute. Or ten. I hope that was worth all two point five million dollars you paid for it."

Anya blushed and giggled as she rested her

chin on his shoulder. "Ask me again in ten minutes."

With a fierce slap, Daniel brought his hand down hard on Anya's bottom. "Respect your elders, young lady."

She yelped in pain before dissolving into laughter. "It was worth every cent of your money, sir."

"Better answer."

Daniel ran his hands up and down her back as Anya nestled into him, her arms still cuffed to the headboard. Maybe he'd leave her there for a little while longer.

"I want you in my collar. I want to own you," he said into her hair. "I want to love you, too."

"Yes, I want that. Please."

He felt something on his shoulder, something wet. Tears. Anya's tears. "Good."

"But under one condition," she said, pulling back to face him.

Daniel gripped her chin and gave her a stern look. "And what is that condition?"

Anya returned the stern stare with one of her one, one fierce enough to rival even The Ouch.

"We burn the jeans."

12

E leanor mounted the back stairs as she headed toward the guest bedroom where she'd sleep tonight. Kingsley would probably be joining them as Daniel and Anya had apparently commandeered the master suite for their own use. Good for them. Kingsley deserved getting kicked out on his ass sometimes. She and Kingsley fought like siblings outside the bedroom, which led to some rather intense encounters inside it. Especially intense since a certain someone took great pleasure in sharing her with his best friend.

Not that she minded. Not one bit.

At the first floor landing she paused when she heard the sound of tears. Downstairs on the main floor she saw Tessa wiping tears off her face as she displayed for a few of the other submissives a black bruise on the back of her thigh.

"Suck it up, Tessa," Eleanor shouted down at her. "It's just a bruise. If you can't handle the beat, get out of the kitchen."

"Eleanor..."

She turned and there was Søren standing behind her at the landing.

He covered her lips with one finger. "Inside voice."

"Yes, sir." She kissed his finger.

The submissives retreated and Eleanor heard a familiar laugh. Two familiar laughs. Daniel and Anya walked through the hallway hand in hand and toward the front of the townhouse. Anya, she noted, walked a little gingerly. Eleanor could only smile at them. They were probably on their way to Daniel's gorgeous apartment, in a hurry to start their lives together.

"Any regrets, Little One?" Søren asked as Eleanor leaned back against him.

"About Daniel? No. Not at all. I care about him, of course. But I know who I belong to, what I want. And he and Anya are great together. He wants kids. So does she. They'll have a good life."

Leaving Daniel after that week together had been unbelievably hard. But as soon as she returned to her life and to Søren's strong arms, she knew that she hadn't really been in love with Daniel, just a little infatuated with the idea of being with someone who could give himself to her completely. She hadn't told Søren how much it hurt that they could only spend one or two nights together a week, if that. But she didn't have to tell him. He'd seen it on her face. And after that week with Daniel, her owner had done everything in his power to give more of his time to her. Sacrificing sleep, risking his calling...all for her.

"They do seem well-suited. A good match. They'll be married in six months. And I've no doubt he'll take all her siblings in."

Eleanor shook her head at the thought of Daniel trying to tame a houseful of five Quebecois kids by day and his feisty French-Canadian submissive wife by night.

"You know," she said turning to face him, "you could have warned me you were going to bid on Anya."

"And ruin the surprise? Little One, the look on your face was truly priceless."

"It would have ruined everything if I'd landed on my ass laughing at you, sir."

It had nearly killed her holding back her laughter when her owner, the Underground's most infamous sadist, had bid on sweet little Anya. She'd had to slap a hand over her mouth just to hold it in. She knew he'd only bid on Anya to help Daniel put on a good show for the woman he loved. Not that Daniel or Anya would ever know that.

She'd started to think of Him lately as some kind of dark angel—terrifying as the angels in the Bible were described but ultimately a force of good. But if He was an angel, what did that make Kingsley?

"*Mon Dieu...*"

Eleanor smiled as Kingsley sauntered down

the stairs looking resplendent as ever in his coat, tails, and riding boots. "What a night. I never should have let Anya keep my fifteen-percent."

Kingsley released a disgusted little French sigh. "It was very sweet of you. Daniel and Anya will be very happy together, because of you."

"Happy and boring," Kingsley corrected. "That man takes all my best submissives and turns them into wives. He's banned from my house."

"Be nice. Daniel deserves a little happiness."

Kingsley reached out and cupped the side of her face. Inhaling she closed her eyes as Kingsley traced the outline of her lips with his thumb.

"I deserve a little happiness. Come, *ma petite*... you can make me very happy tonight."

"Talk to you-know-who," she said, glancing up at Søren.

"We have talked."

Well, so much for her plan to get a little sleep tonight. Anya's besotted laugh carried up to the landing and they watched as she and Daniel disappeared down the hall.

For a moment the three of them stood in silence. Eleanor gazed at Kingsley out of the corner of her eyes. Though they looked nothing alike, only the man she called her owner rivaled Kingsley for male beauty. Kingsley had black eyes that contrasted with her owner's gray ones. Rich tan skin contrasted against pale. Long black untamed hair contrasted to perfectly restrained porcelain blond. But they were quite a team, those two. Especially alone with her. The dark angel hovered her left shoulder. Hell's most charming devil grinned on her right.

Eleanor rolled her eyes. Angel? Devil? Maybe Daniel had been right—maybe she should become a writer. She really needed to start doing something with all these bizarre thoughts in her head. If she did write, it would have to be fiction. No one would ever believe the truth.

Another laugh echoed from the first floor up to the landing. Irina, Kingsley's beautiful Russian dominatrix, strode down the hall with her fingers tucked tight in the collar of a handsome young man. With a small grunt she thrust the young man hard against the wall and shoved her hand down his pants. He closed his eyes as she whispered a vicious order into his ear.

"Daniel..." Eleanor began and then stopped.

"Yes, Little One?"

She swallowed. "Daniel said the craziest thing to me. He said he thought I'd make a great dominatrix. That's crazy, right?"

Her heart pounded hard against her ribcage as Irina brought her mouth to the male submissive's lips and kissed him hard and deep. She pulled away, snapped her fingers, and the young man dropped to the floor. Irina took a step back. The young man crawled forward.

"Don't get any ideas, Little One. Now come to bed."

He kissed the top of her head and started off.

Kingsley ran a possessive finger down the side of her face before he followed her owner.

Below in the hall Irina crooked her finger at the young submissive, and he followed her on hands and knees.

"Oh, Blondie," Eleanor purred the words, her eyes narrowing with desire at the sight of the man on his knees for Irina. "I've got nothing but ideas..."

Eleanor's heart nearly stopped when she realized she'd spoken those dangerous words aloud. But her owner was still walking away, up the steps.

She sagged with relief. Thank God, her dark angel hadn't heard that.

But an infuriatingly French laugh, low and intimate, echoed down the hall, and she knew exactly what that laugh meant.

The devil had heard.

FIN

ABOUT THE AUTHOR

Tiffany Reisz is the *USA Today* bestselling author of the Romance Writers of America RITA®-winning Original Sinners series.

Her erotic fantasy *The Red* —the first entry in the Godwicks series, self-published under the banner 8th Circle Press—was named an NPR Best Book of the Year and a Goodreads Best Romance of the Month.

Tiffany lives in Kentucky with her husband, author Andrew Shaffer, and two cats. The cats are not writers.

Subscribe to the Tiffany Reisz email newsletter to stay up-to-date with new releases, ebook discounts, and signed books:

www.tiffanyreisz.com/mailing-list

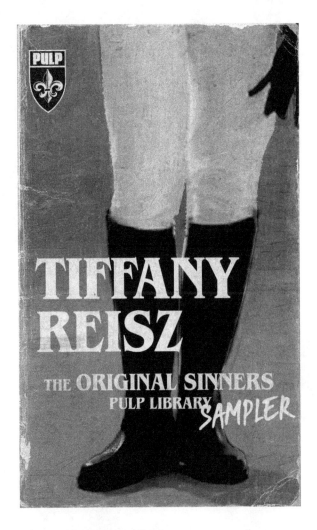

*This **FREE** ebook sampler features excerpts from seven Original Sinners Pulp Library titles. Download at www.tiffanyreisz.com or wherever ebooks are sold.*

SACRED HEART CATHOLIC CHURCH

SINNERS WELCOME